CURSED

A WITCHBANE NOVEL #8

MORGAN BRICE

CURSED

WITCHBANE BOOK #8

By Morgan Brice

eBook ISBN: 978-1-64795-090-3
Print ISBN: 978-1-64795-091-0
Cursed, Copyright © 2025 by Gail Z. Martin.
Cover by Lou Harper and May Dawney.

Darkwind Press is an imprint of DreamSpinner Communications, LLC

1

SETH

"I HAVE WAITED LONG ENOUGH. AVENGE ME!" THE FURIOUS GHOST SENT A frigid wind through the small parlor, sweeping papers from the desk and swaying the curtains. The candle in the middle of the séance table guttered but didn't go out.

"That's why we're here." Seth Tanner had never considered himself a ghost whisperer, but recent situations dealing with angry spirits made him wish for those skills. "We want to stop the man who killed you."

"He took everything from me!"

The spirit of Rod Jennings looked like a tough stevedore in his middle years with a fringe of gray hair around his trucker cap and a muscular body gone soft in the middle.

Seth looked at Alicia Peters, the medium, and saw the strain in her face. Evan Malone, the third person at the séance table, squeezed Seth's hand as a warning to wrap up the conversation. The ghost made himself heard because Alicia lent him enough energy to speak aloud. Seth knew that meant their time was short because she couldn't sustain that for long.

"Who killed you?" Seth needed to hear his suspicion confirmed by the killer's victim.

"Sterling Vernon," the ghost spat, loathing clear in his expression. "I worked on the docks, and I saw what was inside one of his refrigerated shipping crates. There were body parts—not normal butchered cuts of meat. Except, they didn't look like they came from people or farm animals. I swear they were monster meat."

"And he killed you because of what you saw?"

"I didn't know he was behind me. He said something witchy, my heart stopped, and I fell down, dead," Rod replied. "I had a life. A family. That bastard took everything. I want revenge."

Seth could sympathize. He had lost his parents and younger brother to one of Vernon's fellow witches.

Rod's body had been returned from Savannah to be buried in Charleston, making it possible for Alicia to contact his ghost. That was one of many reasons Seth and Evan had stopped in Charleston on their way to deal with the Savannah witch-disciple.

"Is there anything else you can tell us about Vernon that would help us stop him?" Seth asked.

"He got regular shipments of cold crates like that, so if they all had monster meat, he must be doing something with it," the ghost replied

"Do the crates still arrive on schedule?"

"Yeah. Nothing changed—except that I'm dead."

"Alicia can help you pass over if you want to go," Seth offered the irate spirit.

"Not until I've seen that son of a bitch get what's coming to him," Rod's ghost snarled. "You need help nailing his ass to the wall? I'm your man."

"Rest now," Alicia said, and murmured an incantation to release the ghost, who winked out of sight.

She slumped and let go of their hands when the spirit departed. Seth moved to help Alicia lie on the divan while Evan fetched the sports drink and candy bar they had set out to help replenish her energy after the working.

Seth stood a few inches over six feet tall with dark blond hair, chocolate-brown eyes, and an athletic build. Evan, his partner, was just as tall, but he had chestnut hair and hazel eyes.

"We've had witch-disciples selling pharmaceuticals for supernatural creatures and warlocks trafficking shifters and psychics, but monster meat is a new one," Seth said as he and Evan found chairs nearby.

"What do you think it's for?" Evan asked. "Rituals? Spell components? Aphrodisiacs?"

"I don't think I want to know, but we need to find out anyhow," Seth replied. "Sterling Vernon's one of the stranger disciples, and that's saying something." He paused and was quiet for a moment before Evan spoke.

"What's on your mind?"

"Just thinking about Jesse," Seth admitted. "Like always."

A few years ago, Seth and his younger brother, Jesse, had camped out near a haunted bridge on a lark. They intended to spend the night doing silly videos for social media, drinking beer, and hanging out. A mysterious force attacked them, leaving Seth unconscious and killing Jesse. Then his parents died in a suspicious wreck, and the house burned, leaving Seth with a pickup truck, his parents' fifth-wheeler, and the black Hayabusa motorcycle he had bought when he got out of the Army.

No one believed Seth that the causes were supernatural, but obsessive research led to the unlikely truth: Jesse had been a sacrifice for a dark witch in a ritual cycle going back over one hundred years.

"I'm still amazed that for a whole century, no one else noticed the pattern with the deaths," Evan said.

"Cops are trained to look for *human* patterns, not supernatural ones," Seth pointed out. "What doesn't make sense, they ignore as impossible. And don't forget—my parents never mentioned the deaths that happened in my own family. They never recognized the pattern, either."

A century ago, a sheriff's posse hunted and killed Rhyfel Gremory, a powerful warlock. His devoted witch-disciples stalked and murdered the sheriff and his deputies, and used spell work to create a bond to their dead master's spirit, requiring the murder of the eldest male of each of the posse's families. In Jesse's case, the warlock accidentally chose the wrong brother, leaving Seth guilt-ridden as well as bent on revenge.

Seth set out to hunt down Gremory's disciples and stop the carnage, trying to save other families from the heartbreak he had known. He never expected to fall in love with the coven's next intended victim—Evan. Together, they dispatched that warlock, started hunting the rest of Gremory's coven together, and became partners in every way in the process.

Seth watched Alicia to make sure she was okay. She waved off his concern as she ate and drank, regaining her color. Alicia was in her late thirties, plump and unassuming, which made some people underestimate her ability as a powerful psychic and medium. Her black hair fell in waves over her shoulder, a contrast to bright blue eyes.

"Take your time and get your second wind," Seth cautioned. "Megan will whip my ass if she doesn't think I took good care of you." Alicia and her wife, Megan, shared the modest white clapboard house where Alicia did her readings.

Seth turned back to Evan. "We found Vernon's aliases over the years. He's stayed pretty close to the shipping company his father started back in the 1800s. Quite a rise from a sea captain with a single cargo vessel to a small fleet specializing in high-end, unusual cargo."

"*Very* unusual," Evan added. "I figured they'd be smuggling rhino horns, pangolin scales, or tiger bones for ritual ingredients. Not shifter filet or yeti tenderloin." He wrinkled his nose in disgust.

"Makes me wonder who his customers are." Seth leaned back in his chair. "Other immortals? High-status non-humans like vampires, werewolves, and lesser witches?"

"No one's ever been able to pin a smuggling rap on Vernon in all this time," Evan pointed out. "I doubt monster meat is the only thing he's moving in those ships. He's either got protection spells out the wazoo or he's paid off all the right people."

"Probably both," Alicia said in a smooth, low-country drawl, already bouncing back from the energy expended with Jenning's ghost. "He's smart, and he's had time to diversify. Savannah's a major port. If he's stayed in business this long, he's learned to change with the markets."

"Why can't these guys find a way to earn a living that doesn't involve killing people?" Seth muttered. All of the disciples made their fortunes and kept their wealth in decidedly illegal ways. While the underworld warlocks weren't friends, they did work together when power and profit aligned. Between manufacturing and distributing recreational drugs and pharmaceuticals designed for non-humans and shifter trafficking, the remaining dark witches had begun to function more like a cartel than a coven, bound together by their need to sacrifice to their dead master's ghost to retain their magic and immortality.

"Because there's money in murder," Evan observed. "And as we've said before, wealth buys security if you don't want people noticing that you never age or die."

"We've talked with three ghosts so far who were killed by Vernon outside of the ritual cycle," Alicia pointed out, taking another gulp of the sports drink. "They all got too close to whatever's coming and going in those shipping containers. That's good to know, but I'm not sure how it gets you what you need to stop his next sacrifice."

Seth sighed. "I'm not sure yet, either. Evan and I are still working on a plan. We talked with a friend in Pittsburgh on our way here from Cleveland. He knows a lot about lore and magic, and he's got access to an arcane library. That gave us some ideas, on top of what we've learned the hard way dealing with the other witch-disciples."

He and Evan had destroyed six of Gremory's disciples so far, and one had died of indirect causes. That left five more—including Vernon and the witch responsible for Jesse's death. The very first of the coven they fought had sacrificed victims from Evan's family for a century and would have murdered Evan if Seth hadn't intervened.

"I know you're a hot stuff hacker, but Teag's got magic going for him." Alicia set aside her empty bottle. "If there's something to be found online, he'll do it."

Seth grinned. "I'm hoping to pick up some of his tricks. We're going to get together with him, Cassidy, and Rowan, and see if we can figure out Vernon's weak spot and a strategy to take him down."

Vernon made his base in Savannah. Seth and Evan were currently in Charleston, less than two hours away, to confer with friends who knew a lot about stopping monsters and high-powered supernatural beings. They had worked together several months ago to take down the disciple headquartered there and stayed in touch as Seth and Evan pursued warlocks in other cities.

"It's good to see you boys again," Alicia said. "Maybe someday you'll drop by when the world isn't ending."

Seth felt his cheeks heat. "Sorry about that. We've been running at top speed trying not to get killed. But I'm really hoping it won't always be like that." He stole a glance at Evan, who squeezed his hand beneath the table.

"I know, and there's no shame in that. But sometimes we all get so tied up with saving the world that we can't just take a couple of evenings off to have a good time," Alicia replied. "That's important too," she reminded them.

Seth's gaze drifted back to the empty space where the ghost had been. "Do you think our friend is going to be a problem?" he asked, clearly meaning the spirit.

Alicia frowned. "He's been dead for a while and gathering power, but he hasn't tried to hurt anyone. Now that he knows someone is taking his death seriously and planning to stop his killer, I think that will keep him from getting involved. He didn't seem unreasonable, the way ghosts are when they're losing what's left of their humanity."

Once they were sure Alicia wasn't too drained from the séance, they took their leave, promising to keep her in the loop on the hunt for the next witch-disciple.

Seth and Evan stepped out into the bright, clear day. "That was intense." Seth bumped shoulders with Evan. Charleston still wasn't a comfortable place for two men to hold hands in public.

"I can't blame the ghost for being angry," Evan replied. "And I'm squicked out over the possibilities of what Vernon might be doing with monster bits."

"Nothing good, that's for sure. But the quantity seems off for spell components. Maybe he's running a processing plant for hellhound food?" Seth quipped, but as he spoke, something clicked into place in his brain. He and Evan shared a look.

"Oh, my God. What if he's feeding them to something?" Evan looked like he might be sick.

"Just when you think things can't get any weirder," Seth said.

They weren't due to meet with their friends for about an hour, so they took the opportunity for some much-needed downtime. Seth felt like they had been running at full speed since he had rescued Evan, because that was mostly true.

Heroes in movies never need naps, Seth thought. The pace was grueling, and he knew that they needed to slow down so they would be at their best.

Groggy monster hunters don't last long.

Now that they knew about the witch-disciples and their sacrifices, taking time off seemed selfish and indulgent unless they were healing, because lives were on the line. It hadn't helped that some of the witches had moved their sacrifices ahead of schedule to power up in case they were the next to be targeted.

"Hey, where'd you go?" Evan joked to bring him back to the moment.

"Just thinking that we need a vacation," Seth admitted.

"Well, how about a mini vacay? We can take an extra day or so, and Charleston is a top destination," Evan said. "Besides, if it makes your conscience feel better, we'll be researching, so we won't be ignoring the job. There's a lot I've always wanted to see—and photograph—in this town." Evan loved taking photos.

"Oh yeah? Like what?" Seth felt his mood lift at Evan's suggestion.

"For starters, there's Magnolia Plantation—big old house and fantastic garden," Evan rattled off, and Seth had the feeling Evan had already researched the city. "There are some other cool mansions and an art museum. Plus the Charleston City Market, it's got all kinds of interesting shops and awesome food."

Evan's enthusiasm made Seth smile. So much of their time together so far had been steeped in danger and blood. Through it all Evan had been brave and loyal, always having Seth's back. It warmed his heart to hear Evan sound happy and excited about normal things like tourist attractions.

"I'm always up for good food," Seth agreed. "Anything else?"

"History museums and an aquarium, and probably more sites than you could see in a year," Evan replied. "King Street has lots of fun stores, but we're already heading there to see Cassidy and Teag."

They stopped for lunch at a restaurant that specialized in biscuits and gravy, washed down with house-made sweet tea. Charleston leaned into a relaxed pace, perfect for vacationers. Seth suspected the less frantic rhythm was good for the people who lived there as well.

Sipping on iced tea to go when they finished their meal, Seth and Evan made their way slowly down King Street. The historic stretch included trendy shops and restaurants housed in pastel-colored buildings that reinforced the city's oceanfront vibe.

They took their time, window-shopping and remarking on the handmade and luxury items on display, and checking out the menus posted in the windows. Seth loved seeing Evan happy and relaxed, and made a mental note for them to come back to truly enjoy a vacation once saving the world was done.

Evan had his camera, and everywhere they looked, Charleston was picture-perfect. "This city is a photographer's dream," Evan said as he snapped shot after shot.

"Maybe you and your camera need a little 'alone time'?" Seth teased.

Evan rolled his eyes. "Don't let him bother you," he said to the camera. "He's just jealous."

"Well, here we are," Seth said when they reached Trifles and Folly, the store that belonged to their friend and collaborator, Cassidy Kincaide.

"If we lived here, I'd love to be a tour guide," Evan said.

Seth felt a pang. Their quest to stop the witch-disciples was so dangerous, he rarely let himself daydream about what came afterward since they had to survive first.

"You'd be fantastic at it," he encouraged.

"How about you? Got any ideas for what you'd do?"

"We've been so busy I haven't spent a lot of time thinking about it." Seth dodged the more negative aspect.

Evan gave him a look that said he wasn't fooled. "It never hurts to have something to look forward to. Vacations and time off are good, but having an endgame is even better."

"I know I want to be with you, whatever I'm doing," Seth replied with a certainty that went down to his bones.

"The people who are hunting always need researchers. That might be a way to help while staying out of the line of fire."

They were both far too young to actually retire, but the same caution that had led Seth to leave the military after his stint was over pushed him to consider a less dangerous long-term role hunting monsters.

"We've got time to think about it," Seth said. "Got a few more disciples yet to go."

A bell on the door jangled when they walked into the shop. Seth sensed that it was protective as well as welcoming.

Trifles and Folly had been in Cassidy's family for generations. Each new owner took on the responsibility for serving as a nexus of supernatural protection as well as managing a well-regarded shop for antiques and collectibles.

"I wonder if Sorren and Donnelly are around," Evan mused. "They seem to get called out a lot."

"Whatever situation needs a centuries-old vampire and a master necromancer is a job I don't want any part of." Seth repressed a shiver. Sorren, the vampire, protected Cassidy as he had generations of her forebears. Donnelly, the necromancer, had powerful death magic, though he used his power to stop witches with bad intentions. Their specialized skills and broad networks often took them out of Charleston to deal with problems elsewhere on the East Coast.

"Hi guys! Great to see you again." Teag Logan looked up from behind the counter. "Come on in."

Teag was tall and slender with a skater-boy mop of dark hair. As Trifles and Folly's assistant manager, he helped keep the busy shop running when pressing supernatural matters took Cassidy away from her duties. His ability to weave spells into cloth and his background in martial arts proved valuable against bad guys, even if he didn't have Cassidy's abilities as a psychometric to read the history of objects by touching them.

"Cassidy wanted me to remind you about dinner tonight with her, Kell, Anthony, and me." Teag named their respective partners.

"Absolutely. Looking forward to it," Seth replied.

Cassidy returned just then with a tray of four hot lattes. "Sorry I'm late. I popped down the street to pick up some caffeine. Every planning session goes better with coffee."

She pushed a lock of strawberry blond hair out of her eyes when she set down the tray. Seth's eye was drawn to her agate necklace, which complemented her pale complexion. It looked old, and he wondered if it had magic as well as being an heirloom.

"I'll cover the front. Go do what you need to do." Maggie, their part-time helper, assured Cassidy as she moved to the register and front counter. She was over sixty, and her silver-gray hair curled in a flattering bob with sassy blue streaks that matched her eyes.

Cassidy thanked Maggie, and they headed to the table near the back of the store where Cassidy did her readings.

"Fill us in," Cassidy said as soon as they were settled. "I've heard a little from Travis and Brent, but that was mainly that you were alive and settled things with another of the disciples in West Virginia."

Sometimes Seth felt amazed at the network of paranormally-skilled partners he and Evan had managed to find in their quest. Researchers, witches, psychics, mediums, monster hunters, academics—and even a vampire. When he struck out to avenge his brother, Seth believed himself to be alone. While nothing made up for his loss, he treasured the friends and allies he had gained along the way, including Evan, the love of his life.

Seth and Evan took turns recapping their most recent adventure, answering questions along the way. The twelve witch-disciples came from different backgrounds and had varied supernatural abilities. Everything Seth and Evan learned from each encounter added to what they could use against the next one.

"Have you guys ever thought about doing a comic or book series when you're finished? You've run into some epic shit," Teag joked.

"No thanks." Seth waved him off. "My main fantasy is escaping to a not-haunted tropical island and sipping daiquiris in a hammock all day."

"Hey, multiple streams of income can buy a lot of beach drinks," Teag teased. "Just sayin'."

"Don't you actually have some intel for them?" Cassidy said with fond exasperation.

"Yes, I do," Teag replied. "As a matter of fact. I've been working with Rowan to do some digging," he added, mentioning a witch friend of theirs. "The Savannah witch-disciple is a whack-a-doodle, even for that crowd, which is saying something."

"That's a technical term, whack-a-doodle," Cassidy said with a straight face. Teag shot her a joking glare.

"Sterling Vernon is the younger son of a ship captain from more than a century ago. He's a weather mage. He's leveraged those connections to grow an import-export company that specializes in illegal cryptid body parts and derivatives." Teag glanced at the notes on his phone. The disciple's death magic extended his followers' lifespans at the cost of the energy stolen from their victims, so Vernon's extreme age wasn't a surprise.

Seth felt his stomach lurch. "The ghost we just dealt with said Vernon killed him because he discovered a frozen monster corpse in a shipping container."

Teag nodded. "That tracks. Everything Rowan and I could find suggests Vernon uses the bodies for magical and ritual items. But there have been persistent rumors he also caters to 'gourmet consumption' for very specialized tastes."

"I think I'm gonna be sick." Evan swallowed hard. "Are you saying…"

"Just rumors, but the stories have been around for a while," Teag said. "Aside from that, Vernon uses his boats to transport cargo for other witch-disciples, and more than one hunter thinks they're into para-pharmaceuticals and shifter trafficking."

"Lovely," Seth muttered.

"It gets better, or worse, depending on how you look at it," Teag said. "Vernon is part-owner of a popular restaurant in Savannah."

Evan caught his breath, and for a moment Seth feared his boyfriend really might lose his lunch; he looked a little green, but Evan shook his head.

"That's really…disconcerting," Seth said.

"Just wait." Teag seemed to be enjoying the disclosure a little too much, and Seth suspected that Teag and Cassidy had already had time to process the disturbing information.

"Scuttlebutt has it that Vernon also runs an underground restaurant specializing in magical, cryptid, or legendary ingredients whose clients are wealthy immortals, non-humans, and lesser witches," Teag finished.

Seth closed his eyes and took a couple of deep breaths. "So the frozen monster parts the ghost saw might have been headed for the secret restaurant?"

"I guess even other monsters have to eat," Evan managed.

The immortals and supernatural beings who allied with humans generally retained the moral guidelines they had adhered to during their lives. Those whose behavior posed a threat to others had left behind the mores of their humanity or had never been human to begin with. Seth firmly believed that the only reason most people could sleep at night is that they had no idea of the ancient and paranormal creatures who walked among them, hidden in plain sight.

"Rowan and I are still getting details, so I don't have a location yet. It's possible the restaurant moves around, given its nature and select clientele. But as far as I know, at least it's not called 'Hannibal's,'" Teag joked.

"I guess we can be grateful for small favors," Seth replied. "How do we stop him?"

Seth and Evan had already been studying everything they could find about Vernon. Not surprisingly, he was elusive and camera-shy. Very little first-hand information existed, except reviews for his restaurant and the registration for his shipping boats. The photos that had surfaced were poor quality, taken from a distance, and grainy. Seth expected as much. Magic often messed with cameras, and witches frequently used magic to make themselves more difficult to photograph.

Cassidy and Teag exchanged a look. "We've been working on that." Cassidy took a folder from her lap and slid it across the table toward them.

"We found a couple of photos from the newspaper that weren't out of focus," Cassidy continued as they opened the folder. The pictures showed a man who was probably in his late fifties, well-dressed but with a wary look in his eyes. "In both photos, he's wearing a necklace with a charm that looks like a ship's wheel. There's a good chance that's his amulet."

"We also need to find his anchor," Evan reminded them. "We've got to destroy both the amulet and the anchor to stop him."

Seth nodded. The disciples all had objects that served to focus and strengthen their magic. "Identifying the amulet is a good starting point."

"His legitimate restaurant gets good reviews," Cassidy went on. "Classic low-country recipes with unique twists. I doubt he's using monster meat with regular patrons since even with magic, he's got to pass health inspections. That's the kind of thing investigative reporters love to discover."

"They might go looking for meat from unlicensed dealers or endangered species, but not yeti steaks," Seth said.

Teag chuckled. "Yeah, you're probably right about that."

"Vernon keeps a low profile," Cassidy continued. "He has a reputation for being standoffish and keeping his distance, even from the owners of other top restaurants."

"That's a crowd with plenty of prima donnas," Teag pointed out. "It's not a surprise Vernon isn't warm and fuzzy. He gives very few interviews and avoids TV cameras—probably because of the magic."

"Where does the underground restaurant come in?" Evan asked.

"That's been harder to track," Cassidy admitted. "There's a whole history of chefs doing pop-up meals in homes or other locations that don't qualify as a real restaurant or have to adhere to all the regulations. But for the patrons, the sketchy legality and risk are part of the attraction.

"If someone knows the right people, they get on the list. When the chef holds an event, they get word through private channels. It's a very 'need-to-know-someone' thing. There usually isn't a lot of prior notice, which cuts down on the risk of getting raided or having the wrong people find out," Cassidy said.

"In the non-supernatural world, chefs enjoy cooking for a small audience and trying out some new or riskier dishes," Teag put in. "Sometimes they get called 'supper clubs' so it sounds more like a personal social gathering."

"I can see why that would appeal to some people," Seth agreed. "They'd feel special for being in-the-know and getting to try dishes that a chef hasn't added to their main menu. It would be a status symbol to be invited."

"And for supernatural beings, it's less status than safety, especially if the menu has to be…unconventional," Teag added. "There's trust involved between the clients and the chef, but then again, if your guest list is made up of monsters, that's a lot of incentive not to blow their cover."

"There have been some famous busts of supper clubs over the years. Outside of the supernatural community, the attraction is usually illegally hunted game meat, risky things like puffer fish, or using meat or products from endangered animals. It's hard to believe some of the things people will take a chance on eating just for bragging rights," Teag said with an expression of distaste.

Seth had done some research along those lines on his own, and it had nearly ruined his appetite for dinner.

"And his regular restaurant hasn't had any allegations of walking on the wild side?" Evan questioned.

Cassidy shook her head. "Nothing we found in the health department reports or news searches. I doubt even magic could cover up anything too weird."

"I didn't find anything, either, and that was before I knew to look for monster meat," Seth said.

"Can I just vote against eating there, even so?" Evan said, making them all chuckle.

Seth reached over to pat his arm. "I'm totally fine with that. We'll have plenty of choices—Savannah's a foodie haven."

"What do you know about weather mages?" Evan asked.

"Like most magic, weather witching can take a lot of forms," Cassidy replied. "Sometimes it's one step up from someone getting advance warning on a change for their lumbago or sore toe. On the lowest levels, it's being able to use magic to accurately predict the weather. On the higher levels, it's actually influencing that weather, like calling up a storm or redirecting the path of one. A really powerful weather witch is dangerous to everyone."

"Yikes," Evan said. "I'd rather not get hit by lightning if we can avoid it."

"Rowan is working with her coven on countering storm magic and creating protective amulets to help neutralize the danger—think of the necklaces as a supernatural lightning rod," Cassidy replied. "And you don't have to take on any of the witch-disciples that seem too powerful. No one expects you to be martyrs or to do this all on your own. There's always another way to tackle the problem."

"These witches have been doing what they do for a century," Teag pointed out. "I understand that you don't want anyone else to get killed, but if the difference between taking them on successfully or not is the time to build a team, then it's worth the wait."

Seth and Evan had discussed that point many times, and they had learned to rely on allies instead of trying to handle situations themselves. Even so, there had been some close calls.

He thought about their conversation earlier that day, about getting 'out of the life' as friends in monster-hunting circles called it. When Seth first started on his quest, it had been steeped in the need for absolution, atoning for Jesse dying in his place. Then he fell in love with Evan and had a reason to live after the last of the witch-disciples was gone. He had no intention of giving up that future, no matter how strong the impulse was for revenge.

"I know." Seth gave a side glance at Evan. "And this isn't a suicide pact. We have plans for a happily-ever-after, but it would be nice for that to be in a world where the witch-disciples aren't still taking sacrifices."

"That's totally understandable," Cassidy said. "It's just that this whole thing about stopping supernatural threats—it never ends. And it's easy to lose perspective, especially when there's a personal loss behind it. Good friends remind each other to step back and breathe from time to time," she added with a smile.

"Thanks," Seth said and meant it. Finding Evan was more than he ever dreamed possible, and he definitely wanted a long life together. But it would be satisfying—and safer—not to leave unfinished business behind.

"Why don't you two go enjoy the city, and maybe by the time we have dinner this evening, I'll know more from Rowan," Cassidy said. "Make sure you go to the market, even if you've been there before. The merchandise changes all the time."

Seth thanked them, and Cassidy promised to text him if anything urgent came up. Back on the street, he looked at Evan.

"You're the one with the list. I'm following you."

THEY STARTED WITH THE CITY MARKET AND, ON THEIR SECOND PASS, found a remarkable number of vendors and cool items that they had overlooked the first time. Living in an RV cut down on the space for decorative items, but they still found a set of kitchen towels as a souvenir and some seasoning blends that leaned into Charleston's foodie reputation.

With just an afternoon to wander, they meandered around The Battery, stopping to enjoy the fountain, and commented on the vivid colors of Rainbow Row's houses. A brisk walk brought them to the aquarium and the Fort Sumter visitor center, where they easily whiled away the time before dinner.

Evan had a great time getting photos as the light changed, giddily indulging his passion. Their trips often either weren't as photogenic or didn't allow time for taking pictures, so Seth enjoyed seeing Evan getting a chance to have fun.

"I'm always surprised by something at an aquarium," Evan admitted. "Some of those fish look like they came out of a sci-fi movie."

"That was fun," Seth agreed. "The museum was interesting...and sobering. I remember reading about Fort Sumter when I was in school, but the museum makes it real."

They had barely begun to explore the historic district before it was time to head to meet the others. Tucked away down a side street, the locally-owned seafood restaurant looked like it might live up to its reputation.

"It's got to be hard running a restaurant in a city like Charleston," Evan said as they waited for the others to show up. "Attracting tourists is good for business. But get too touristy and the locals don't come, and the people who live here year-round keep a place in business."

"The good ones seem to manage," Seth said. "And Cassidy would definitely know."

The others showed up minutes later, talking and laughing. Seth and Evan shook hands with Kell and Anthony, whom they had met the last time they were in Charleston to deal with the city's own witch-disciple.

Kell Winston, Cassidy's partner, a paranormal investigator and filmographer, was tall and lean with light brown hair and blue eyes. Anthony Benton, a lawyer, was Teag's husband, with blond hair and blue-eyed boy-next-door good looks. By unspoken agreement, they kept the conversation light, veering away from the case or the supernatural. Cassidy and the others filled them in on new things to do in town and urged them to plan on spending time now or later to explore and take time off.

Seth and Evan caught them up on places they had stopped as they traveled, with the others adding their favorite tourist traps and historic locations.

"The epic road trip part is pretty awesome," Evan admitted. "Even if dealing with the problem when we arrive isn't."

"Once you take care of business in Savannah, there are some fantastic restaurants and museums," Anthony said. "Assuming you're not in a hurry to leave."

"Won't know about that until we get to that point," Seth replied. They usually beat a hasty retreat after defeating the local witch-disciple since loyalists were likely to hold a grudge even if they lacked similar magic mojo.

"I completely understand," Kell said. "Then come back to Charleston and we'll give you the grand tour. My group visits all kinds of really interesting old places, but I'm not always in a hurry to go back, depending on how the evening went."

Kell ran the Southern Paranormal Outlook and Outreach Klub, also known as SPOOK, a local ghost-hunting group that explored the many haunted places in Charleston and surrounding areas. Seth had heard some of Kell's stories about encounters with ghosts, and they weren't for the faint of heart.

Evan and I go looking for trouble to settle old murders. I can't imagine doing it for fun, but it seems to work for Kell.

Teag's husband, Anthony, was a lawyer with one of the city's long-established firms. "I never have the right kind of stories to tell," Anthony said. "Courtroom drama isn't usually nearly as fascinating as they make it look on TV, and the 'good stuff' is all privileged."

When Seth first started hunting with Evan and acknowledged the attraction between them that bloomed into love, he feared that their chosen quest of stopping deadly witches didn't lend itself to a long-term relationship. Seth had started out hell-bent to avenge his brother, and at the beginning, he hadn't worried about what might come afterward.

Falling in love with Evan changed everything, giving Seth a reason to want to survive their quest and plan a future. Sometimes the idea of an "after" still caught him by surprise.

We need to spend more time planning that. Something to build toward, improbable as it might seem.

As if he guessed the drift of Seth's thoughts, Evan slipped his hand over to squeeze Seth's leg beneath the table.

After that, Teag and Cassidy kept them entertained with stories of some of the more unusual objects that came into Trifles and Folly. Although they handled more than their share of cursed, haunted, and supernaturally-tainted objects, most of the pieces were merely old, some more valuable than others.

The evening passed quickly, and Seth's spirits lightened from the combination of good company and great food.

Before they went their separate ways outside, Cassidy laid a hand on Seth's arm. "Come by the shop tomorrow morning. I got a text from Rowan, and I think she'll have her part of the information pulled together by then. I also have two people in Savannah that I want to introduce you to: Nash and Caden. They know the score, and they can be helpful with the 'project.'"

Seth thanked her, and he and Evan said goodbye as the group broke up for the evening. Since the night was cool, Seth had uncoupled the truck from their RV instead of taking the motorcycle.

"Cat got your tongue? What are you thinking?"

Evan was quiet on the drive back, and Seth's question pulled his attention from the passing scenery. "I had fun. It's good to get a chance to just be with friends when we aren't running for our lives."

"True." Seth wondered where Evan's thoughts had strayed.

"And I love seeing other couples like Teag and Anthony—like us—who've been together for a long time and make it work."

"Yeah, that makes me happy too." Seth knew something was niggling at Evan, but his partner would share it in his own time.

"I don't think guys like us, who've seen the kind of stuff we've seen, can ever go back to a completely normal life," Evan said. "But I don't want to hunt forever. When we're done with the disciples, I'll be happy for us to walk away from hunting for good. Finish the quest, slay the dragon, and live happily ever after." He sighed. "I don't want to push our luck."

"I get it." Seth's Army training hadn't completely prepared him for fighting a supernatural foe, but it provided a perspective and a level of experience that a civilian like Evan didn't have or want. "I don't want to hunt forever either."

Their earlier conversation had stayed in Seth's mind, and he found himself thinking about what life without the quest to stop the witch-disciples might be like. They still had several more adversaries to go, but now, Seth felt like the end was almost in sight.

"That's all," Evan said. "I don't have anything figured out, but the ideas keep circling in my thoughts. What to build toward. What later looks like."

Seth reached over for his hand in the dark. "I love that. And I want to be with you forever, no matter what we're doing. As for the details, we'll figure it out. But I agree, having a later in mind makes the rough parts easier."

None of Seth's wards or alarms around the RV had tripped, but even so, he and Evan circled it cautiously, just to be sure. Relieved, Seth unlocked the door and powered down the protections for them to enter.

Evan surprised him by pulling him close as soon as the door was locked behind them and pressing him against the wall. He slipped a hand up Seth's cheek to draw him into a slow, deep kiss.

After a second or two, Seth caught on and kissed back with quiet passion. He loved the taste and smell of Evan, the feel of his hands, and the weight of his body. Seth had no doubt that Evan was the only one for him, and Evan had made it very clear many times that he felt equally committed.

"How about we skip the movie and popcorn tonight and take this to bed?" Evan rumbled.

"What did you have in mind?" Seth asked, already breathless.

"Anything. Everything. Nothing. I just want to be wrapped up in you," Evan replied.

"That sounds like the best plan I've heard all day." Seth let Evan lead him by the hand.

2

EVAN

Evan woke slowly, tangled in the sheets, with Seth's arm thrown across his midsection. Their snug travel trailer home had a bed large enough for two grown men, for which he was eternally thankful.

He listened to Seth breathe, content with the warmth of the bed and having Seth near and safe. Last night's slow, indulgent lovemaking let them say with their bodies what they sometimes struggled to put into words.

When he had been a bartender in Richmond, before he met Seth or learned about the supernatural, Evan didn't have a clear plan for the future. He liked bartending well enough but had no intention of still slinging drinks in twenty years. Evan had been considering his options when everything got turned upside down, and Seth had rescued him and destroyed the witch-disciple that had preyed on the men in his family.

"Penny for your thoughts."

Evan turned to see Seth watching him with a fond look. He snuggled closer. "Just enjoying the downtime. It's nice to get a break and have a chance to catch our breath."

Seth combed his fingers through Evan's hair. "I heard what you said about after." His voice was a low, sleepy rumble. "And I want that."

Evan touched Seth's cheek. "Glad I made a difference." Seth's admission wasn't exactly a revelation, but it made him swallow hard to hear his partner speak so matter-of-factly.

"A huge difference." Seth leaned in for a light peck on the lips. "We're damn good together. Thank you for signing on to my crazy quest."

"The witch-disciples have been killing people for over a century—including my family. No one else stopped them. When we're done, there won't be any more sacrifices, and those victims will be avenged," Evan replied.

On rough days, Evan wished they could walk away and hand off the task to someone else. As he got to know others in the supernatural community, he realized that nearly all the other monster hunters had lost someone and got into hunting for vengeance. Those who lasted the longest shifted from pursuing a vendetta to accepting that someone had to protect civilians from paranormal threats.

"I know there are some guys who never want to do anything besides hunt," Evan said quietly. "They can't let it go. I don't want to keep pushing our luck once the job is done. That doesn't mean we can't be a resource for lore, magic, or séances. But maybe we can stay out of the line of fire."

Seth pulled him close. Evan took a deep breath, inhaling the smell of sweat, sex, linens, and a faint touch of Seth's cologne. "I'm fine with that. Milo and Toby consult, but they don't do much active hunting. I never asked, but I always suspected it was for those very reasons. They're pretty good role models."

Milo and Toby were retired hunters who had taken Seth in and mentored him when he first started tracking the witch-disciples. They owned an online security company and handled paranormal issues on the side, supporting researchers and hunters across the country.

Evan leaned in to kiss Seth again, warm and sweet. He drew back and sighed. "Guess we should get a shower and breakfast. Cassidy and Rowan thought they'd have more info for us, and we need to head to Savannah."

Seth stole another peck on the lips. "We can save time and get ready together."

"Works for me."

While they wouldn't both fit in the RV's shower, the bathroom hand job was worth it. They made a quick breakfast of coffee and toast with peanut butter before heading to Trifles and Folly.

Teag met them at the door of the antique shop. "There's a fresh pot of coffee in the breakroom," he welcomed them. "Cassidy and Rowan are in there."

They greeted their friends and topped off their travel mugs before settling in at the séance table.

"Thanks for helping, Rowan," Seth said. "I hope you've got some good stuff for us."

Rowan was in her early thirties with shoulder-length blonde hair. Her girl-next-door look hid that she was a powerful witch and the leader of a local coven. "Good to see you two again. Cassidy brought me up to speed. I think I have some things that will help."

She lifted a black drawstring bag from her lap and carefully laid out its contents on the table: bone and silver talismans.

"I know you've got protective bracelets from Teag and tracking spells. There are a couple more charms here for you to pass on to the witch's target and their significant other. And I have two amulets here, one for each of you, that will complement your bracelets." Rowan slid the necklaces toward Seth.

"I've written out some spells that might come in handy on the cards for you to memorize." Rowan indicated a silk bag. "Weather magic seems big, but it's important to remember that even a powerful mage is unlikely to conjure up a huge storm. That requires too much juice and calls attention.

"Most of the time, they use things like a localized downpour, high winds, or a sudden freeze—things that can cause a real problem but aren't going to have weather reporters flocking in with camera vans." Rowan chuckled.

"These spells should be well within your ability, Seth. Sometimes the simplest things pack the most punch. The defensive spells drain the hostile energy away to make it harmless. A few are protection spells that can be used over and over. They won't hold off everything, but they can buy you time and give you a chance to get to shelter—or take your shot," she said with a knowing look.

Seth's magic was a small gift that gave him limited abilities to do simple, rote spells. Rowan and others had taught him some spells that could be done by non-witches who possessed a spark of power, exceptional focus, and strength of will. That had come in handy many times to save their skin.

"Just remember—weather magic is like any other kind of spell," Rowan told them. "It takes a lot out of the witch who casts the spell, especially if they intend to hold it for a long period of time or have the magic affect a large area. You can use that against Vernon by distracting him with your attacks and forcing him to use his energy for protection."

"Do you think he can throw lightning?" Evan asked something that worried him since they found out about Vernon's specialty.

Rowan sighed. "Maybe. That's pretty advanced because it requires the caster to control and redirect a great deal of power. Some high-level witches can do it, and I know the disciples have had over a century to practice. It's also something that puts the witch in as much danger as the target. If the witch miscalculates, they absorb the lightning themselves. Needing to put protections in place drains time and energy from their attack, so they can't just throw bolt after bolt, despite what you see in the movies."

Evan would have preferred to find out that the idea was a myth, but natural limits to keep Vernon from hurling lightning like a pissed-off Zeus brought a measure of comfort.

"I know you held off telling Cassidy and Teag everything until I could be here," Rowan said. "Now that you know more about Vernon, fill us in on his next victim."

Seth leaned back in his chair and took a sip of coffee. "Paxton Miller is the target—he prefers 'Pax,' by the way. Young chef with big dreams. Owns a food truck and has gotten very good reviews for quality comfort food."

"After I read the reviews, I was pretty hungry," Evan admitted and the others laughed. "Seems he's got a way of tweaking familiar recipes that makes them special without being too different."

"His long-time boyfriend, Tony Spencer, is a musician, and he often plays near where the food truck is parked," Seth continued.

"Pax's father disappeared twelve years ago," Evan put in. "Which matches with the disciples' sacrifice schedule."

"Pax still supports his mother and a younger sister," Seth went on. "Tony left a bad family scene and started busking and playing in small clubs. Now, he's a local club regular. He and Pax have been together for a couple of years. I wouldn't be surprised if they opened a restaurant with live music down the line."

"We think Vernon has already connected at some level with Pax through the restaurant community," Evan said. "If you didn't know what Vernon really was, it would look like a good thing for an established restaurateur to mentor an up-and-coming young talent."

"Except he's grooming Pax to be dinner for the next cycle," Seth said in a sour tone. "And Vernon has to have heard about the other disciples that we've killed. He might move the sacrifice forward to boost his power if he thinks we're coming for him."

"That's a legitimate concern," Rowan agreed. "Then again, Vernon has a pretty big ego. We already knew that since Gremory died, his disciples don't really get along. Just because some of them were worried, Vernon may feel strong and superior and figure he doesn't need to be concerned or change his schedule."

"I'm looking forward to proving him wrong," Seth said with a wolfish glint in his eyes that worried Evan.

How do you balance a quest for justice with any sort of sanity? This is like that show with the two guys who drove around in the big car fighting demons. Makes for great TV but sucks as a job description.

Crazy as their life was, Evan had no intention of leaving Seth, despite the danger. *How many times do you get a chance to do something that really matters? We'll change the future for twelve families and all their descendants—including ours. That's worth the danger.*

"I'll see if I can dig up anything else," Teag offered. "If I don't have something by the time you leave Charleston, I'll VPN it to you." Ensorcelled encryption worked wonders to protect sensitive files about paranormal subjects.

"Thanks," Seth said. "There's never too much information, and you never know when it's a little thing that will make all the difference."

"I've been working on witch connections for you in Savannah," Rowan said. "I've got a contact for you—Kinsley Martell. She's well-regarded in the supernatural community there and has been a practicing witch long enough to be proficient. Most importantly, she draws on elemental magic, which is earth, air, fire, and water, which makes her more versatile if your witch-disciple is a general weather witch. And she has a necromancer friend that Donnelly vouches for."

"Sounds good," Evan said. "If Vernon's been in Savannah under one name or another, how do we know he doesn't have influence over the covens?"

Rowan frowned. "I realize that most of your experience has been with a twisted group of men who chose to follow a dangerous cult leader. But most witches are very independent. We pride ourselves on not taking orders well. And while we respect talent and experience, covens are usually pretty egalitarian."

"I didn't mean any offense—" Evan hurried to add.

"None taken," Rowan replied. "I doubt Vernon has invested much energy embedding himself in the local magic scene—sounds like he'd think he was too good for common witches. It would also be hard for him to hide his immortality. But I'll use my sources to verify. I don't want to guess wrong and find out that he's got lackeys or fans eager to curry favor."

"How do we get in touch with Kinsley?" Seth asked.

"I've already given her your number." Rowan picked up her phone and texted Seth. Kinsley's contact information popped up on his phone. "There. You're connected. Let her know when you get to Savannah, and then you can figure out what to do from there."

"Thank you so much. We're glad for any help," Evan assured her.

"Which brings me to Nash and Caden." Cassidy finished her coffee and set the cup aside.

"Nash Arden runs a pub and B&B. He knows about the supernatural, and he's a medium, which is why he didn't go into the family business of being a funeral director," Cassidy added with a raised eyebrow.

"Yeah, that would be awkward." Evan shuddered.

"Caden Brady is a police detective, which can come in handy," Cassidy told them. "He's also psychometric, so he can sense the history and magic of objects by touching them, also helpful."

Evan appreciated the idea of psychometry and knew it was Cassidy's gift, but he was glad not to have the ability himself. The idea of reading so much information from casually touching an object gave him shivers and made him think of movie characters who always wore gloves.

"He and Caden have been a couple in real life for ten years now, working together to stop supernatural threats," Cassidy continued. "They usually stick to run-of-the-mill haunts and minor paranormal creatures, not big guns like Vernon. But they're good backup, and while they know the area and players, you'll still be taking the lead."

"I don't want to get anyone killed," Seth said. "Maybe we should leave them out of this."

Cassidy shook her head. "I've already spoken to them, and they're all in. Actually, they're pissed that Vernon has been killing people in their backyard, so to speak. As for the risk...it goes with the job. There's no such thing as a simple haunting or exorcism."

Evan knew that from experience. Creatures could turn out to be more powerful than expected, or a shift in the location or circumstances might change the balance. He and Seth had narrowly escaped several situations that went wrong at the last minute.

"We've had small abilities turn out to be the game-changer," Evan reminded Seth. "We can usually use all the help we can get."

"I'll keep looking for contacts and information and feed you what I find," Cassidy assured them. "And in a pinch, it's about two hours for us to get to Savannah, so don't be shy about yelling for help if you need it."

"Will do," Seth promised.

Evan knew that his partner accepted assistance from their friends in the supernatural community, but was reluctant to endanger others. While Evan appreciated Seth's protective streak, it often reminded him that helpers with special abilities could dramatically reduce the risk of going up against someone as powerful as Vernon.

He finished his coffee and set the empty mug aside. "We should probably get on the road."

They thanked Cassidy, Kell, and Rowan, sharing hugs and promising to be in close touch. Seth and Evan had ridden the Hayabusa from the RV park where they left the truck and camper.

They didn't say much until they loaded the motorcycle onto the back of the RV and got on the highway. A benefit of taking their lodging with them was that packing to leave was never an issue.

"Okay, talk to me," Seth said once they were on the highway and Charleston was in the rearview mirror. "What's on your mind?"

"I hope Kinsley is a good fit as a witch partner," Evan replied. "I'm not as hesitant to bring others in on the fight if it ups the odds of success."

"I know," Seth admitted. "It's hard for me to ask for help. I may be overprotective."

Evan snorted. "Ya think? Just a little, maybe?"

Seth rolled his eyes. "Okay, okay. I am. You've helped me see that. I don't want to put other people in danger. But I also don't want to put you—us—at unnecessary risk. I won't turn down the help."

Evan squeezed Seth's thigh. "Thank you. Because the real win is getting to live happily ever after when we send those evil sons of bitches to hell."

"I know we probably won't have a chance to sightsee once we get to Savannah." Seth kept his eyes on the road as he spoke. "But is there anything you'd like to at least walk by? Or come back to, after the coast is clear?"

They couldn't afford to let the witch-disciple get the jump on them, so Seth and Evan usually got to the location just a few days before they intended to go after their quarry. Whether they could go back later depended on how much of the disciple's coven remained and if they'd left behind any trouble with the police.

"They have their own historic City Market, an old fort, and a really cool-looking cemetery," Evan said since he had been jotting notes, just in case. "There's a trolley tour—I love those. And some well-preserved old houses, of course. Forsyth Park looks beautiful for a nice walk. Plus a cathedral. And a ton of great places to eat."

Seth chuckled. "I knew you'd already have it all worked out. I hope we get to see at least some of those things, if not now, then maybe someday."

"There's the restaurant that Vernon owns, the legit one, anyhow," Evan said as they drove past.

"Looks pricy," Seth observed. The marquis read "Legacy" in gold lettering on a dark green background, suggesting an upscale experience and a British pub vibe.

Evan grimaced at the bleak humor of the name, given the immortal witch's history of passing his properties to his newly reinvented self with every cycle. A large ship's wheel was also emblazoned on the sign. "Guess it's going for more of a cozy, private feel," Evan noted. "Even if a crazy, serial killer witch runs it."

"Let's just hope that none of the 'exotic' meat is going to this place," Seth said.

"It gets good reviews." Evan scrolled on his phone. "Expensive, nice date night, quiet, intimate. And apparently, the food is good. Steak and seafood with a low-country twist."

"If we didn't know the story behind who runs it, I'd be tempted to try it. Been too long since we had a nice night out." Seth didn't glance away from the road, but his soft smile made Evan's heart beat a little faster.

"Sounds great to me, but the monster meat is a hard pass," Evan agreed.

"Let's find the RV campground Caden recommended and uncouple the truck," Seth suggested. "Once we get set up, we can check out Nash's tavern."

The Savannah Shores RV campground was slightly north of the city, with a beachfront on the Savannah River, not the ocean. "It's not exactly Savannah or shores," Seth said with a chuckle as they pulled in.

"We weren't going to get to hang out in the sand anyway," Evan pointed out. He couldn't help sounding wistful.

"We'll take a break before tackling the next disciple and go somewhere we can feel the sand between our toes." Seth put his hand on Evan's thigh, eliciting a smile from Evan, who liked that idea. "And we'll make sure you get plenty of time to take pictures. Savannah's supposed to be just as photogenic as Charleston."

"Let's just put this case to bed and walk away safe." Evan crossed his fingers for luck.

The attendant at the gate said they were expected and gave them the number to find their spot. Evan looked around as they drove.

"Well-lit, tidy, looks like it's maintained well," he noted. "Some of those buildings look vintage."

"Eighties nostalgia," Seth said. "People who want to relive when they were kids, or share that vibe with their children or grand-children."

"Looks like somewhere I've seen in movies," Evan replied. "I'm sure that's a big draw for families."

"Cassidy said that Caden was friends with the owner. Since he's a cop, I'm hoping that bodes well for security." Seth followed the signs and lot numbers until he found the spot they had been assigned. It had more elbow room than many places they had parked, as well as a picnic table, Adirondack chairs, and firepit.

"If we ever come back, we should keep this in mind," Evan agreed. "We passed a sign for a canteen and snack bar."

They had gotten good at settling in, opening the bump-outs, and were hooked up to the utilities in record time. Seth uncoupled the truck and set the alarms to protect the RV and motorcycle, then put down a salt circle and magical protections. Evan entered the address of Nash's pub, Mystic, in his phone, and they headed back toward Savan-nah, where the bar sat at the edge of the historic district.

"I know we can't ride the bike everywhere, but it's a damn sight easier to park." Seth angled the truck into a spot that provided a clear line of sight to the bar and an easy getaway.

"And cold. Don't forget cold," Evan teased.

"That, too. Although not as bad down here as back home," Seth replied.

Mystic took up the bottom floor of an old brick building with large windows and a tastefully lit sign. The bar had a comfortable neighborhood hangout vibe, and Seth felt comfortable immediately when they walked in. Dark wood paneling and brass fixtures gave an upscale touch without seeming stuffy. Framed pictures showed city life in Savannah throughout the years.

"Let's go in and see if Nash is working. Maybe Caden will drop by after his shift." Seth locked the truck as they walked away.

Memorabilia about the Savannah music scene—band photos, concert broadsides, and framed albums—covered the walls. A small stage at one end sat empty at the moment, but the sign on the wall announced upcoming acts.

"Hey." Evan gently elbowed Seth to get his attention. "Check out the set list. I guess Pax's boyfriend is more than a casual musician."

"Tony Spencer," Seth murmured, pointing to the familiar name on the lineup. "I wonder if we'll get the chance to hear him play."

"Teag said that sometimes Tony busks near Pax's food truck, so maybe he'll be playing when we're staking out the location," Evan replied.

They headed for the bar and waited for someone to take their order. Evan recognized the bar owner from the photos Cassidy and Teag had shared.

Nash Arden appeared to be in his early thirties, with reddish-blond hair and scruff. His green eyes sparkled as he bantered with customers while shaking a cocktail. A gold ring glinted on the third finger of his left hand. When they got closer, Evan could see that his nametag read, "Nash—Owner."

A second bartender worked the other end of the very busy counter, and servers relayed drink orders from the customers seated at tables.

Evan felt a pang of nostalgia since he had been a bartender in Richmond before Seth saved him from the witch-disciple. He had enjoyed the work, although he never planned to make it his career. The freelance projects he did now satisfied his creativity and suited his new nomadic lifestyle.

"What can I get you?" Nash asked when he worked his way down to them.

"You brew your own beer?" Seth asked.

"Sure do," Nash replied with pride. "Best in Savannah."

"Two glasses then of your favorite," Seth ordered. "I'm Seth, and this is Evan. Some mutual friends may have mentioned we were coming to town."

The look in Nash's eyes turned assessing, although his smile held. "Yep. Been expecting you. I can't talk right now, but give me half an hour, and I'll have someone to cover for me." He turned away to pull their drinks and slid them across the bar. "Enjoy."

Seth and Evan turned their backs to the bar and looked out over the small restaurant. It felt genuinely cozy, without the forced ambiance of tourist traps. The patrons ranged from young professionals who looked like they stopped in after work to retirees and travelers.

Evan tried to listen in on the conversations near him at the bar, but didn't pick up anything out of the ordinary.

Before long, Nash returned. "C'mon. My folks can cover for me for a while. I've got a back table where we can talk. Caden will be here soon, once his shift ends."

They took their drinks and followed Nash to a small booth set off by itself, angled so that Nash could watch the restaurant but far enough from other tables to afford privacy.

"Glad you're here," Nash said once they got settled. "Cassidy briefed me on your background and what you've been doing. How can we help?"

"I don't know yet," Seth replied. "We just got to town, and we're getting our bearings. Tomorrow we'll observe the guy who's the next target and figure out how to approach him."

"I wish we could just introduce ourselves, explain the danger, and have him and his boyfriend just ride off into the sunset so we can deal with the threat, but it never works that way," Evan said. "I was a target, and I didn't believe Seth until I got kidnapped to be the next offering."

"We've also got to figure out what serves as the anchor for the bad guy's magic, because we're going to have to destroy it," Seth added.

Seth slid a photo of Pax and Tony across the table. "Pax is the target. Tony's his partner."

"I recognize these guys. They come in pretty often for dinner. Tony plays in our live music rotation. In fact, he's playing tonight. They seem like good folks." Nash frowned as if thinking. "If it's a genera-tional sacrifice, how come the target doesn't realize it?"

Evan extended his senses, getting a feel for Nash's abilities as a medium.

"You and I are used to seeing ghosts." Evan met Nash's gaze and saw the man's surprise when he took Evan's meaning. "That makes it a little easier to accept things out of the ordinary. Regular people don't have that. And the disciples have had a century to learn to cover their tracks. They know how to hide in plain sight and create plausible explanations for the disappearances and deaths. Normal folks don't think this kind of thing happens except on TV. I wish they were right." He paused. "I didn't believe Seth when he first told me and almost got us both killed."

"I've lived in this town all my life and certainly never even caught a whisper of something like that going on. Despite being in the Bible Belt, Savannah has a fairly large and vibrant occult and paranormal community. Witches, mediums, and people with special insight like Caden. This is the South. It's one of those things everyone knows about and no one mentions," Nash said.

"Talk to people who grew up here for long, and they know someone with a sixth sense or who was a ghost whisperer, or could put a root on someone who vexed them. Officially, the Church disap-proves, but in practice, there's nothing they can do about it," Nash added.

"Hi, sorry I'm late." A blue-eyed, dark-haired man walked up to stand beside Nash and laid a hand on his shoulder, a proprietary touch that spoke volumes. Evan noticed the matching gold ring on the newcomer's left hand. "I'm Caden."

"I'm Seth, and this is my partner, Evan," Seth introduced. "Glad you could join us."

Caden slid in beside Nash. "For what it's worth, it was a quiet shift at the station tonight."

"Quiet is good," Nash clarified. "Caden's a detective with the Savannah Police Department."

Cassidy had told them that Nash was a medium and Caden had psychometry, the ability to read the history of objects by touching them. He wondered how Caden had managed his psychic ability with the demands of his job and didn't envy him the struggle.

"I did some digging on the name you gave me—Paxton Miller," Caden said. "He's clean, not even a parking ticket for his food truck. According to official records, his father died of a heart attack while deer hunting, and a search party found his body in the woods. Paxton's grandfather was killed in a car accident when his truck went into a ravine, and he was found a few days later in the wreckage."

Nash had gone silent, with a far-away look in his eyes that Evan recognized. Evan felt the presence of the ghosts as well, but sensed that they gathered around Nash, so he let the other medium take the lead.

"My sources say that isn't the whole truth," Nash said quietly, referring to the ghosts. "They don't remember all the details, but they agree that there was a man and a strange light and that their bodies were moved from somewhere else."

Evan and Seth exchanged a glance. "That's actually very helpful," Seth said. "It squares with the idea of the coven and the ritual. They've made an effort to cover their tracks. I'm guessing no one questioned the deaths at the time?"

Caden shook his head. "Not from any records I could find. Deer hunting kills a surprising number of hunters as well as deer, and the ravine where the truck was found is infamous around here as a 'dead man's curve' for accidents. If someone was covering up dark deeds, they knew what they were doing."

"Vernon's had a century of practice," Evan said with a touch of bitterness. "And the ritual doesn't have to leave marks depending on how it's done."

"I also checked offline deed records that hadn't been digitized for the names you gave me," Caden added, referring to Vernon's past aliases. "Currently, he owns a restaurant, warehouse, an import/export business, and his home under his name, as well as cars and at least one cargo ship."

Seth nodded. "We found those. But we could only go back so far online to see if he bought properties in the past under other names and still held onto them. It could be handy to know."

Evan knew Seth suspected that the coven's meeting place and the location for the ritual sacrifices were likely to be somewhere Vernon owned or controlled.

"Most of the old properties don't exist anymore," Caden said. "Not surprising. Some of them burned. Most were repurposed or torn down. For the ones that were sold, I checked the buyers' names against the alias list, in case he was selling to his new persona. I only found one property like that, an old turpentine plant from the 1920s."

"Interesting," Evan said. "It's just sat empty since then?"

Caden shrugged. "Apparently. It's in an out-of-the-way location for current traffic patterns, and there hasn't been enough development around it to put a premium on the land."

That sounded like the perfect spot for Vernon and his witches to work their ritual, where they wouldn't be noticed or disturbed. Magic could hide their coming and going for sporadic gatherings, especially since the big event would have more than a decade between recurrences.

"I just emailed you the address," Caden said. "Funny thing—I checked for drone or aerial photos and nothing usable showed up. Anything in the search results fuzzed or fizzled in that section over the plant and only in that section."

Evan sighed. "I'm not surprised. We've talked about whether it would make sense to get a drone for surveillance or recon, and that's the problem—magic isn't always camera friendly." He grinned. "But we still bought one and I'm itching to give it a try."

"There are old photos from about sixty years ago," Caden said. "I copied them from the archive and emailed them to you. It doesn't seem like the building itself has changed much. It's sat empty since it closed in the late 1960s, but it hasn't fallen into disrepair, so someone is taking care of it."

"Thank you," Seth said. "It's a huge help to have someone familiar with the territory."

"What's the plan from here?" Nash asked. Evan noticed that the bar was getting busier, and he knew that Nash wouldn't be able to spare time for them much longer.

"We're going to try out the food truck tomorrow, see if Tony is playing nearby, and chat them up," Evan said. "Get the lay of the land."

"It might help to accidentally-on-purpose run into them here tonight and talk to Pax while Tony plays," Seth mused. "Wouldn't hurt to meet up in a neutral safe space and have Nash recognize us—builds trust. After that, we'll play it by ear."

"We're here if you need backup." Caden dug several business cards from his wallet, which he handed to Seth. "You know how to reach us."

They shook hands and Nash went back to the bar, with Caden following, taking an open stool to hang out.

"Let's just get dinner here," Seth suggested. "I'm tired from the drive, and I don't feel like cooking. And then we'll be here when Tony plays."

"Suits me," Evan agreed.

He went up to the bar and came back with menus. "Nash says that the music starts in about half an hour," he reported. "Tony is the second one up, so we can chill for a while and snack on appetizers and then dinner."

"Sounds like a plan." Seth scanned the menu. "Get any recommendations from Nash?"

"I know burgers aren't original, but I saw one on someone's plate, and it looked really good."

"You want to do the ordering? You know how I like mine." Seth handed back the menu. Evan took them back up front and talked to Nash, then returned with another beer and sat.

"Figured I'd take one for the team since you're driving." He lifted his glass in a mock toast to Seth. "Nash is on board with the plan, and he's fine with us just hanging out and munching."

The crowd at Mystic seemed laid back, a mix of ages. From their clothes, Evan guessed they ranged from business colleagues dropping in after work to locals and tourists.

A server brought a plate of fried green tomatoes and blue crab dip with house-made chips along with soft drinks. Evan hadn't realized how hungry he was until he smelled the food.

"Wow, that's really good," Evan said after trying some of both dishes.

"Definitely better than the standard bar food," Seth agreed.

They paced themselves so that they could be finishing up when it was Tony's turn to play. That would allow them to bump into Pax on their way out without seeming contrived.

Their burgers came just as the first musician stepped up to introduce himself. His playlist of mellow folk tunes had the patrons nodding agreeably and clapping between songs.

"This is dangerously awesome." Seth nodded toward his burger. "I'd be in trouble if we could eat here regularly."

Evan agreed, even though he usually ordered something a little lighter. "I'm glad I went for it. When it looks that good, it's worth trying."

Since they were waiting for Tony to play, dinner was a leisurely affair, something rare that felt almost decadent. They often ate quickly on the road or made a hurried dinner in the RV after a busy day. Evan loved the change, even if it was part of working the case.

"Almost like a date," Evan remarked.

"I was thinking the same thing." Seth paid the bill, and they waited for Tony to take the stage next.

The first guitarist wrapped up his set to appreciative applause from the diners. Evan had spotted Tony coming in about fifteen minutes earlier and hanging out in a corner near the front. Just like his photo, he had shaggy brown hair and a trimmed beard.

When the first musician cleared the stage, Tony took his place with his guitar and music. The way he hooked up to the bar's sound system made it clear he had performed there before.

"There's Pax," Seth said.

Evan recognized the man from his photo—tall, slender, clean-shaven, with short ginger hair. Pax had taken a seat at the bar where he could cheer on his partner.

"Hi, everyone. I'm Tony, and I hope my songs make your evening a little brighter." He sat and began to play. His first two songs were soft rock favorites, a comfortable background for dining.

"Come on." Seth plucked at Evan's sleeve. They got up and made their way toward the front but paused at the bar behind Pax like they wanted to hear at least one more song before leaving.

"He's really good," Evan commented to Pax, just a friendly comment to a stranger.

Pax grinned. "Tony's freaking fantastic. Is this the first you've heard him?"

"Yeah, we just got to town," Evan replied. Seth stayed close behind him, ostensibly focused on the music but tuned into the conversation.

"You picked a great bar to start with." Pax never took his eyes off Tony. "The food is terrific, and I'm pretty partial to the music." While he didn't come out and admit that Tony was his partner, his encouraging smile made it clear that they were at least close friends. Evan understood the need to maintain plausible deniability for safety's sake.

"Guess our friend gave us a good tip," Evan said. "Got any suggestions for us?"

Pax pulled a card from his wallet and handed it to Evan. "I run the Peachy-Cue food truck over at the Market. It's barbecue with my signature peach sauce. There are a bunch of trucks with pretty much everything anyone could want, but I'm biased about mine being the best." Pax gave a broad grin. "Plus Tony and other musicians play at lunch."

"That just went on the must-do list." Evan saw Seth nod out of the corner of his eye. "By the way, I'm Evan and this is Seth."

Pax turned enough to shake hands before returning his attention to Tony and clapping as a song came to an end. "Great to meet you. I hope you have fun in Savannah and come by the truck."

"Please tell Tony we enjoyed his music," Evan replied. "And we'll definitely try out the barbecue."

Evan didn't have a good excuse to chat longer and didn't want to set off any stalker vibes, so they slipped out at the end of the next song.

He and Seth headed outside. They made a check of the area around Mystic to make sure no one might be lying in wait for Pax or Tony, but didn't see anyone suspicious.

"Well, that accomplished more than I expected," Seth said as they walked to the truck.

"Our cases don't usually have such good food," Evan agreed, deliberately misunderstanding and bumping Seth's arm.

Once they were on the road, Evan looked at Seth while his partner drove. "Thoughts?"

Seth shrugged. "That went well. I like Caden and Nash. Got good vibes—not that I'm surprised considering who recommended them. Definitely helps to have local boots on the ground. Between Caden's connections and knowing who to ask, he saved us at least a day's work and gave us a possible ritual site." He paused. "Doesn't hurt to have someone who can help cover our tracks, if we need it."

"I liked them too," Evan replied. "Nash's ability with the ghosts is real. I'd love to see Caden's psychometry in action, but I don't envy anyone that gift. I wouldn't want to hear the gossip from every antique. I don't know how Cassidy manages."

"Running an antique shop as a psychometric has to be tough, but it's her family business, so I guess she's figured out how to make it work," Evan added.

"I imagine Caden has figured out how to tamp it down to do his job with the police," Seth said. "I would think that's one of the first things someone learns with an ability like that."

"How about Pax and Tony? At least now when we stop by the food truck, it's not a cold call," Evan said.

"They seem nice and unguarded. They've really got no idea what's coming at them." Seth sounded tired, like the danger weighed on him. "I hate to spoil that, but it's the price of saving their lives."

"I know what you mean. And once you know, you can't 'un-know.'" Evan sighed. "It's been a long day. Let's get a good night's sleep and start fresh tomorrow."

"Can we stop for donuts and coffee in the morning? I want donuts."

Evan laughed. "Absolutely. Sugar and caffeine are required for saving the world."

By the time Seth was out of the shower the next morning, Evan had located a local coffee shop whose pastries had a devoted following, according to the online reviews.

"These are even better than I expected," Seth moaned as he bit into his second donut.

"The coffee is better than average too," Evan agreed. "And I like the vibe of the place." The Coffee Spot had a kitschy décor showcasing everything coffee-related, including posters, vintage mugs, china cups, grinders, and photos.

They chose a table in the back where they wouldn't be in the way and spent time planning where to go next.

"I figured we'd drive around and get the lay of the land before we hit the food truck for lunch," Seth said. "At some point, I'd like to see Vernon's restaurants."

"Do you think we can go inside and look around?" Evan asked. "Either of the restaurants might be a hiding place for his anchor."

Seth thought for a moment and shook his head. "Seems like a big risk. We can't be sure whether or not he knows who we are. If he does, we'd be walking right into his hands."

Evan sipped his coffee before replying. "Okay, I see that. But maybe Nash and Caden could at least go to the regular restaurant. The ghosts might tell Nash if there's a powerful magical object inside, and Caden's psychometry could validate the power. Then it's just up to us to steal it."

"That could work without putting them in too much danger," Seth agreed. "It's a public restaurant, so it's not strange for them to be there. If Vernon knows Caden's a cop, he might tread carefully. And right now, there's no reason for him to connect them with us."

"The monster meat restaurant is tougher." Evan drummed his fingers on his cup. "But maybe Nash could marshal some of the ghosts to check it out when it's closed. Kinsley might be able to get a read on anything with strong magic if the spirits find something that could be the anchor. Or maybe one of them has a friend who could pay a visit."

Seth nodded. "I like those ideas. They could work without too much risk. And I agree that the restaurants are likely hiding places. That's hoping it's not hanging in his bedroom or in his office."

Evan shook his head. "I guess that's possible, but I think that he's likely to have it somewhere he can draw on the magic. Let's see what we find, and if the anchor isn't there, we'll come up with new ideas."

Seth's knee nudged his under the table. "Before, after, and in between, I'm fine if you have some things on your sightseeing list, plus time to take pictures. Maybe after lunch, we should drive by where Pax and Tony live and get an idea of how vulnerable it is."

Evan knew it was tough for his hard-charging partner to build in off-time and appreciated Seth's willingness to indulge his touristy interests. "That all sounds good."

"Savannah's a modern city, but I love how much of its history is still here," Evan said as they drove. "Some places are better than others at growing but also holding onto their heritage." He found himself enjoying the drive around the city even though they were doing reconnaissance.

The morning flew by, and his grumbling stomach reminded him that breakfast had been a while ago. "Probably time to go looking for Peachy-Cue," Evan said.

Even with traffic, it didn't take long to find the lot where Pax had his food truck. Peachy-Cue sat in a row of vendors lined up in a lot cordoned off from other parking. Picnic tables added a festive feel.

The truck stood out with bright yellow paint and a red and yellow striped awning over the ordering window, with a prominent menu board. Hungry diners lined up at each of the trucks, while others enjoyed their food and conversation at the tables.

At one end of the lot, a small raised platform served as a stage with an amplifier, a stool, mic, and music stands. A sound system guaranteed that the performances could be heard by the patrons of the trucks but wouldn't spill far beyond the boundaries of the lot.

"There's Tony." Evan nudged Seth. Tony fussed for a moment to plug into the amp and arrange the stool and stand to his liking.

"Hello, everyone!" the musician called out to the crowd. They responded like old friends, giving Evan the impression that the regulars were familiar with him as well as with the trucks.

"For anyone who doesn't know me, I'm Tony Spencer, and I'm

going to be playing for the next little bit. Sit back, enjoy the day and your lunch, and relax—you're on Savannah time now."

Tony went right into an upbeat acoustic classic he hadn't played at the bar the night before. He soon had folks in the audience nodding along. Seth and Evan got in line for food, and the tangy, rich aroma made Evan's stomach growl.

"Interesting menu." Seth poked Evan with his elbow and nodded toward the board on the side of the truck where the choices were painted in bold letters.

"Chopped pork sandwich with choice of our own Peachy-Cue or Carolina Gold sauce. Fried pickles. Candied bacon." Evan read aloud and noted the serving sizes and combos. The rest of the board listed drink options.

"Pick one and I'll get the other, and we can do the same with the pickles and bacon," Seth suggested. "Gotta say, I'm intrigued."

The truck had a line of people waiting. All of the vendors were still busy, and the live music added a festive feel to the gathering.

When Seth and Evan got up to the window to order, they saw two men inside alternating taking orders and filling plates.

"Told you we'd come by for lunch," Evan said when Pax smiled in recognition. "Everything on your menu looks great."

"Glad to see you made it. What can I get you?" Pax seemed relaxed and in a good mood despite the heat wafting from inside the truck and a non-stop line of customers. "Choosing one of everything is always a good move," Pax joked.

Seth gave their order, and Pax nodded approvingly. "We'll have that ready quick. What brought you to Savannah?"

"Here on business," Seth replied. "Although it's tempting to stay for the food."

Pax grinned. "There's a lot of good 'cue in the city, but in my completely biased opinion, I think ours is the best."

It didn't take long before their order was ready. Seth carried a tray to one of the open picnic tables, and they settled in. Evan hadn't realized how hungry he was until he dug into the food.

"He wasn't kidding about the sauces." Seth polished off both halves along with his share of the pickles and bacon. "Those are addictive."

"Yeah, I'm tempted to get seconds, even though I know I shouldn't," Evan said ruefully.

The trucks were busy, but plenty of tables meant Seth and Evan didn't feel pressured to leave right away. That gave them the chance to sip their drinks and appreciate Tony's music.

"He's good. I give anyone credit for having the balls to perform in public, especially in a setting like this." Seth nibbled his last piece of bacon.

"The crowd loves him. Pretty clear that he plays here a lot and that there are plenty of regulars eating the food." Evan enjoyed Tony's upbeat song choices that had him tapping his toe.

The food truck lot was set back from a busy sidewalk, with an open-air market on one side and shops on the other. That made for plenty of foot traffic, especially since Evan guessed at least some of the buildings also housed offices.

"Hey, over there," Seth said with a nod.

Evan followed his line of sight and saw a man standing at the edge of the food park. Nothing about the way he was dressed set him apart from the diners or the passersby, but he just stood and stared at the people without appearing to be particularly listening to the music.

"The ghosts don't like that guy," Evan said in a low tone. "I'm picking up on some kind of magic, not witch-disciple level mojo, but he's not a mundane."

"I wonder if he's here to keep an eye on Pax," Seth replied. "I've got an idea. Cover me."

With that, Seth grabbed a handful of flyers for discounts at the various trucks from the end of the table and headed toward the stranger. Evan watched closely, ready to spring into action if it looked like his partner needed backup.

Seth approached the dour stranger with a big grin. Evan couldn't hear what was said, but Seth tried to foist off coupons on the man and invite him to try the trucks; the man backed away, looking annoyed and angry.

"No idea whether he's working with Vernon, but at least he left,"

Seth said as he came back to the table. "I don't like being stared at while I eat, and I figure other people don't either."

"Just because he's a creep doesn't mean he's connected to one of the disciples," Evan said quietly enough not to be overheard. "Maybe he's looking for someone to rob. Or he just hates music." He didn't really believe either option.

"Coincidences are never coincidental," Seth said.

"You should put that on a T-shirt."

Seth rolled his eyes. "You know what I mean. We come here to protect Pax, and there's a creepy stalker guy hanging out and staring at him. It's got to mean something."

Evan only realized that the music had stopped when Tony walked up to their table. "Pardon me, but I saw what you did, making that jerk go away. Thank you."

Seth gestured for Tony to join them, and he sat down on the end of the bench. "He gave me the creeps staring at everyone, and so I figured offering him coupons would move him along without starting a fight."

Evan knew that Seth had a few weapons hidden on him if it came to needing to defend himself, but he felt grateful that the situation hadn't escalated.

"He keeps coming around, and he never buys anything," Tony confided. "But since there's no law against standing there and watching people eat, we can't call the cops. Everyone's seen him, but no one knows who he is or why he's interested."

"He comes every day?" Evan asked, and Tony nodded. "Same time?"

Tony shook his head. "Times vary, but it's always the same guy. Started about a month ago. I don't remember seeing him before that." He sighed. "I'm sorry. Pretty sure you two are first-timers. I didn't mean to make you think we've got a creeper problem."

"Don't worry, we've already fallen in love with Savannah," Seth assured him. "And we enjoyed your music last night at Mystic."

Evan could see the moment Tony made the mental connection. "I thought you looked familiar. I saw you talking with Pax. I love playing there. Nash takes good care of us."

"Are you from the city?" Seth made small talk even though they knew the answer.

Tony hesitated, as Evan expected he would. From what their intel told them about the pair, both Tony and Pax had fled bad family situations to strike out on their own in Savannah, meeting once they were in the city.

"No, but it's definitely home to me now," Tony said with a smile that reached his eyes. "Crazy musician chasing a dream and all that. So far, it's been working out—cross your fingers for me!"

"The trucks do a good business," Seth observed. "Is it this busy all the time?"

"Pretty much, except when it rains. We're not in peak tourist season now, it's even busier then. They work hard. It's hot in those trucks," Tony said.

"We really loved the barbecue, especially the peach one," Evan added.

Tony flashed a proud smile. "That's Pax's family recipe. He left home with that and a couple hundred dollars in his pocket and did all right for himself. Of course, I'm probably biased. He's my boyfriend."

Tony hesitated as if waiting for their reaction, and Evan knew not everyone in Savannah was open-minded. To set Tony at ease, Evan moved his hand to brush against Seth's knuckles.

"We didn't really introduce ourselves. I'm Evan, and this is my partner, Seth."

"Business partner?" Tony gave them an assessing look.

"That and life partner, too. Package deal," Evan replied with a smile.

Tony nodded as if answering an unspoken question. "Cool." He glanced at his watch. "Oops, break time is over. I need to go play. I hope you'll come back. All the food is good, but Pax's is the best."

With a wave and a smile, Tony headed back to the stage, stopping to greet other diners along the route. Evan glanced toward the Peachy-Cue truck and saw Pax watching Tony fondly.

They listened to a couple more songs, but without ordering more food, Seth and Evan didn't have an excuse to keep taking a table. Evan dumped their trash in a bin and gave Tony a salute as they left the lot, heading toward the nearby shops.

"That was pretty damn awesome," Seth remarked.

"The whole setup is great. I'm glad to see all the trucks doing so well. Having live entertainment is certainly a draw, but people wouldn't come back if the food wasn't good," Evan replied.

"I never thought peach and barbecue could go together, but that was amazing."

Evan chuckled. "Didn't know you were quite that much of a food-ie," he teased.

"Just calling it like it is." Seth looked at Evan as if assessing his expression. "What are you thinking? I doubt it's about fried pickles."

"They were good too, and the candied bacon was damn near orgasmic," Evan replied.

"I wouldn't go quite that far—"

"But I was just thinking that it's going to be hard to get Tony and Pax to believe us," Evan continued. "I mean, it always is. It's a crazy story unless they've heard rumors about their *real* family history."

There's an immortal killer witch who wants to sacrifice you to his dead master so he and his coven can level up. We're monster hunters, and we're here to save you.

"We'll have to figure out a way to cut through the skepticism," Seth replied. "We've always managed before."

"I know, but I still worry," Evan replied.

"How bad are the ghost crowds?" Seth asked as they walked back to where he had parked the truck. Evan had told him what it was like when they were in Charleston, another city with a long history of being known as haunted.

"Distracting," Evan replied. "They're everywhere. Most of them are repeaters, so no consciousness, but I keep feeling like I need to say 'excuse me' for walking through them even though they're too weak to actually manifest."

"You take it in stride pretty well."

Evan shrugged. "Been doing it all my life, although I think my ability to see and talk to them has gotten stronger with all the practice since we've been doing what we do."

"It's like there's an invisible city on top of what most people see."

"That's a good analogy, except that the people are from every time period. So native people, early settlers, colonists, sailors, and everyone else from the last three hundred and fifty years. Sort of like a costume party gone wild," Evan replied.

Evan could see their truck as they turned a corner. Seth was choosy about where he parked, careful that he couldn't be easily boxed in either by accident or on purpose. The truck sat where they had left it, first in the row of curbside parking spots where pulling out would be easy.

Seth slowed and so did Evan. "What's up?" Evan asked.

"Something's not right," Seth growled.

Before Evan could ask more, a man stepped out from behind a parked van and took a swing at Seth. A second man came at Evan from the other side of the vehicle.

He had no idea whether the attackers wanted their wallets or were hired by Vernon to scare them off, but Evan didn't have time to wonder. Training took over, and all the sparring he and Seth did between jobs paid off as Evan evaded his opponent and landed a punch to the jaw that set the man back a pace.

"Leave town." The man swung again and landed a bruising hit to Evan's shoulder.

"Who hired you?" Evan asked while evading another punch. Out of the corner of his eye, he saw that Seth was fighting hard to hold off his own opponent. The street was quiet, but sooner or later someone was likely to notice a brawl in broad daylight.

At least so far, the two men hadn't pulled weapons.

"Stay out of it," the man snapped. "What happens here is none of your business."

A police siren screamed, not far away. The two men ran. Seth and Evan gave chase, but the next intersection opened to a busy street, and they lost sight of the strangers in the crowd.

"Let's not stick around to explain to the cops." Seth unlocked the truck and pulled away before the squad car arrived.

Evan didn't realize he was holding his breath until they were back in the flow of traffic. His shoulder ached, but he knew it could have been much worse. "Did they hurt you?" he asked.

Seth's grim expression and locked jaw let him know how angry he was. "I might have a bruise on my jaw tomorrow," Seth replied, and Evan could see where a red spot was starting to bloom. "I missed the worst of the punch, but he definitely intended to put me on the ground. How about you?"

"Got hit in the shoulder, but it could have been worse. Probably have a mark."

"Did they say anything to you?" Seth asked. "Because he told me to leave and stay out of stuff that wasn't our business."

"That's what the guy said to me too," Evan replied. "What game is Vernon playing? He could have used magic to ambush us, or the toughs could have shot us. I'm glad that didn't happen, but I don't understand."

"Jumping us is easy to pass off as an attempted robbery," Seth said. "Murders in broad daylight get more attention. Even if Vernon has the police in his pocket, that kind of thing is hard to cover up, and it wouldn't play well in a tourist town."

"Do you think he knows we're the ones who killed the other witch-disciples? He seems to see us as an annoyance instead of a threat," Evan mused.

"I'm fine with being underestimated." Seth glanced over to Evan. "Can you grab my phone and pull up the first text message? I sent myself Pax and Tony's address. Then put it in the GPS."

Evan's hands shook in the aftermath of the fight as he took Seth's phone. Seth seemed calm, but Evan knew that battle training and military experience helped Seth deal. That wouldn't stop him from seething inside at the attack.

"On the downside, if he sent goons after us, it means he knows who we are and figured out it's related to the ritual." Evan called up the directions and put the phone in its holder on the dashboard. "And we've made contact with Tony and Pax. Now all we have to do is get them to believe us."

3

SETH

"We've figured something out to make it work every time so far," Seth said. "I honestly think Tony might not be a hard sell, considering how suspicious he was about that creepy guy. I wonder if he has some degree of psychic sensitivity, even if it's latent."

"I hope so. It would be a big help to have him on our side to win over Pax," Evan replied.

As they drove, Seth kept an eye out for the man from the food lot or their attackers, but they seemed to have vanished. "If Vernon has his goon keeping an eye on Pax, then he means to make his move soon," Seth said. "He's not going to have someone stand there every day for a year."

"Yeah, I thought of that," Evan replied. "Either we got here just in time, or Vernon heard we were coming and moved up his timetable, making it our fault Pax is in danger early."

"That actually works in our favor. We're forcing Vernon's hand, and hurried magic tends to be poorly done," Seth responded.

They made sure to drive past the food lot again. A different musician played oldies on stage, but Seth caught a glimpse of Tony hanging out around the tables near Pax's truck.

"While we know where they both are, I thought we could get a look at their house," Seth said. They followed the GPS and found a tidy bungalow on a quiet side street that looked well-tended, and he pulled over with the pretext of studying directions so they could get a better look.

"They're renting, so that limits some of the magical protections," Evan mused. Seth knew that locations that were public—as in, not owned by the person who was the spell's target—were more difficult to ward because the linkage wasn't as strong.

"Not to mention that we can't just hop the fence and start chalking strange sigils everywhere. I'm betting Tony has already made friends with the whole block. Someone would notice."

They pulled away before their pause drew attention and turned down a side street to get a look at the rear of the house.

"If anybody comes in from the back, he'll have to go through someone else's yard to get to Pax and Tony's," Evan pointed out as they drove away. "Which requires more magic to avoid notice, and the neighbors' dogs barking. I also spotted a couple of security cameras."

"Okay, so Pax is reasonably safe for now," Seth agreed. "But it will be a lot easier if we can convince both of them to go to a safe house in Charleston and sit out the big fight than trying to lock down a suburban neighborhood."

"Agreed, but that's probably going to be a tough sell. There's no telling whether Pax has someone to cover for him if he can't cook for a few days. Shutting down the truck means their income takes a hit, and that goes double if Tony isn't playing," Evan pointed out.

"Yeah, but we gotta give it a shot." Seth took a route that drove past Legacy, Vernon's legitimate restaurant. "Looks like Vernon is doing all right for himself."

The location looked as upscale as the reviews and menu prices suggested.

"The local foodie blogs gush over how Vernon helps fledgling restaurateurs get their projects off the ground and participates in all kinds of fundraisers and food service education scholarship programs." Evan looked up from his phone. "I wouldn't be surprised if he's already reached out to Pax in some legit way to establish a connection and win his trust."

Seth wrinkled his nose like he smelled something bad. "That's just…sick. Like playing with your food."

Still, it would make sense for Vernon to keep an eye on Pax, knowing that the sacrifice time was growing near. Getting attention from a local superstar chef would certainly lower any natural wariness Pax might have, especially since the vast difference in their status ruled out any fear of competition.

Providing helpful tips or even dropping positive comments about Pax's food and the truck would move Vernon from being a total stranger to an acquaintance and make it that much more difficult for Seth and Evan to sell Pax and Tony on wild claims about supernatural danger.

"Turns out I was right," Evan said as Seth headed back to the RV park. He waggled his phone back and forth since Seth couldn't look away from the road long enough to see whatever was on the screen.

"You usually are," Seth conceded with a fond smile. "What now?"

"Articles about Vernon being one of the judges in a Savannah 'best food trucks' event, posing with Pax as one of the winners," Evan replied. "The prize included media coverage, a cash award, and a mentoring session with one of the judges. But the photo of his face is blurry. There's another picture where Vernon is standing with Pax next to the truck, and Pax is holding an engraved plaque. Vernon's looking away, so it's not a good image."

"Fuck. Vernon isn't just a local food god, he's someone Pax has actually met and who did him a couple of good turns," Seth replied. "That means Vernon's won his trust, at least a little bit, and demonstrated that he's not a threat."

"Not a threat right then," Evan agreed. "Kind of like an assassin cozying up to the target, who has no idea there's been a hit ordered."

The Mob analogy was a little too close to the mark for Seth's comfort, given the dysfunctional family of the witch-disciples. Memories of stopping the first disciple from killing Evan still haunted Seth's dreams.

"Anything interesting about Legacy?" Seth asked.

"If we talk Nash and Caden into going there to scout for the anchor, we ought to pay for their meal—and it won't be cheap," Evan observed. "Vernon also has a thing for old-fashioned ships' wheels. He used a fake one on his sign, and one is printed on the menu and all his ads. He was a ship's captain back in the day. That pendant he wears is probably his amulet. Do you think a wheel might be his anchor?"

Seth considered the suggestion. "Maybe. But would he keep it in his restaurant? Seems like people would notice if it disappeared from time to time."

"Worth checking, but I agree," Evan replied. "On another topic, I've been poking around some of the seamier corners of the internet to see if I could find anything about the underground restaurant beyond what Teag discovered."

"How seamy?"

"Dark Web stuff. Definitely bad online neighborhood sort of thing," Evan replied. Their research often took them to questionable locations —real and online—to find occult and arcane information.

"Anyhow, I found a food blog that was either written by someone in the supernatural know or who wasn't exactly human. It could have been completely made up, but it didn't feel that way," Evan said. "The reviews were stomach-turning, but if any of it was true, then Savannah's reputation holds true for monsters. And Vernon's secret restaurant is top of the heap."

"Restaurants come and go all the time," Seth mused as they parked next to the RV. "It would be a perfect business for someone to drop out of sight every twenty years or so and reinvent themselves. In his case, he could launch a new restaurant and lay low for a while to not be recognized, and no one would think it was strange." He paused. "Did it have a ship's wheel logo?"

"Not that I saw. It had very little online presence. It barely had a name, 'Our Place,'"

"Catchy and bland. I guess the creatures who need to know already do." Evan frowned as he scrolled on his phone. "Here's something: Vernon is accepting an award at a public event tomorrow night for innovative restaurant leaders. If we hid in the audience and didn't try to get close to him, maybe he wouldn't notice." He smirked. "You could always wear a fake mustache."

"Funny. Not," Seth replied, but couldn't help smiling. "I guess it depends on whether he is on alert for us to show up. If he's not looking for us, and we don't attract attention, it might work. And he's hardly going to strike us with a bolt of lightning in front of a whole room full of witnesses."

"You hope," Evan replied. "But I think it's worth the risk. Even with today's media, he manages to avoid a lot of photos or video, and what does exist is always out of focus."

One of the difficulties with immortality lay in keeping others from noticing, especially if the witch wanted to stay in the same general location. Gremory's witch-disciples had all staked out their territories and built businesses that sustained their wealth in those places. In the old days, evading pictures was easier. Now, the witches tended to rely on magic to smudge the evidence and make it more difficult for someone to recognize them, assuming anyone aside from Seth and Evan knew to look.

Seth's phone pinged. Evan checked it since Seth was driving. "You got a text from Kinsley, Rowan's witch friend."

Seth nodded. "Good. I was hoping we'd hear from her soon. Let's get inside and I'll call her."

They drove back to where the RV was parked and made a thorough check, but none of their protections had been disturbed. Seth wasn't sure whether that meant Vernon didn't know where they were or if he just chose not to tip his hand just yet.

Once they were inside, Seth returned Kinsley's call. "Hi! This is Seth Tanner, returning your call. Okay if I put you on speaker so my partner, Evan Malone, can hear too?"

"Hi, Seth and Evan. Yes, speaker is fine." Kinsley's voice filled the kitchen, deeper and smokier than Seth had expected. "Rowan has told me a lot about the two of you and your...project. Gotta say, I'm intrigued. Everyone in Savannah has heard about Sterling Vernon. People who get that kind of success usually have a bit of magic to them, acknowledged or not. But I did not realize he was a witch of power or had his unfortunate side business."

Her phrasing made Evan snort and Seth chuckled. "That's one way to put it," Seth replied.

"Rowan said she gave you plenty of charms and protections and fundamental defensive spells," Kinsley went on, "and that you knew how to use them. But I'm guessing you're expecting bigger problems?"

Seth leaned against the counter while Evan poured still-hot coffee from a thermal carafe for both of them.

"Having backup means we have less trouble stopping the witch-disciple, as in, we don't nearly get killed," Seth told her. "Magic and muscle both make a difference. Vernon's going to have his coven, and they'll be expecting to power up from the ritual, so they won't take kindly to having it interrupted."

"What happens when you stop the sacrifice?" Kinsley asked.

"The witch-disciple dies, and his coven loses its power." Seth didn't try to sugarcoat the situation.

"You two play for keeps."

"Gremory's disciples have been killing people every twelve years or so for a century," Seth pointed out. "Including my brother and relatives, Evan's family members, and more. The ritual keeps them immortal, so the deaths would just go on and on. Seems like offing an evil bastard and saving all those people is a good trade."

Rowan had thought Kinsley would be an ally, but if she was squeamish about the reality of the situation, Seth needed to know before they were in a life-or-death battle.

"Slow your roll," Kinsley said. "I'm on board. Rowan and Cassidy laid it all out, and witches like Vernon give the rest of us a bad name. I just needed to hear it from you."

"You'll help?" Evan asked, looking hopeful.

"Yeah. I want that scum and his monster meat joint out of my city," Kinsley replied. "I think I've got more witches and maybe some muscle to help out too. Plus a friend who's a necromancer, if that would come in handy. Want to meet for breakfast and plan a war?"

Kinsley suggested a place run by a coven member's family where she felt they could talk safely without being overheard. Evan noted the address as Seth repeated it, and they thanked Kinsley before hanging up.

"Well, that might be another piece falling into place," Evan said.

"The sooner, the better." Seth hadn't been able to shake the feeling that the clock was ticking on an unknown danger. Dispatching Vernon and leaving town couldn't happen fast enough to suit him. He didn't share his sense of foreboding with Evan in case his imagination was running wild, although experience had taught him to trust his hunches. That meant being extra careful.

That evening, Seth cooked tacos while Evan scoured local media sites for anything about Vernon that they might have missed.

"I've come across a few articles praising Vernon for how he shuns the limelight and avoids the spotlight for his good deeds," Evan reported in a wry tone. "That hasn't stopped him from insinuating himself into the restaurant industry in the city. He turns up everywhere. He just manages to avoid photos most of the time, or makes them blurry."

"Hard to be a recluse and run a restaurant," Seth replied without turning away from the stove. "It's a people business."

"More so in Vernon's case maybe than for most," Evan joked.

"Ew. Don't spoil my appetite."

"Sorry. Couldn't help it."

"Vernon's got to have mortal helpers," Seth said. "Is there any info on who runs the place when he's not around? Or the head chef, business manager, maître d'?"

Evan nodded. "Yeah. Teag and I found some info. Looks like a very loyal, small group that has been with the restaurant for a long time. Nothing that suggests they have supernatural abilities, at least nothing that would keep them from mingling with regular people and going around in the daylight."

"No vampires."

"Can't guarantee that about the wait staff or the kitchen crew, but not the top people who usually deal with the media when Vernon 'isn't available.'" Evan framed the last few words in air quotes.

"I wonder if he has them under a compulsion or just won their everlasting loyalty by bailing them out of a jam," Seth mused.

"Could be either," Evan said. "I also texted Nash to see if he was free in the morning before the pub opens. I want to see if he and I could contact the spirits of Pax's father and the other men who died from the witch-disciples. Maybe they can give us some inside information to help Pax believe us."

"It's worth a shot." Seth put the finishing touches on the tacos. He carried plates to the table as Evan closed down his computer to make room.

"Those smell amazing. Maybe we should think of having a food truck when this is all over," Evan joked.

Seth gave him a look. "No. Once we deal with the witch-disciples, I'm done with having to haul our home—or our business—around. We'll pick a place, get a house…and go from there."

It bothered Seth sometimes that they didn't have a detailed idea of what to do after their quest was finished. Part of him shied away from making firm plans out of a superstitious fear that doing so might jinx their odds of surviving the task. Earlier in his relationship with Evan, he had worried that planning for a future together might be moving too fast.

Now that they were solidly a couple and had dispatched a majority of the witch-disciples, the possibility of an afterward didn't seem so far-fetched.

Seth worked as a white-hat hacker for Milo and Toby's security company when he wasn't using his skills to break into the witch-disciples' accounts. Evan's passion for photography and his talent for design led to starting his own graphics company, and helped with the occasional need to create fake documents for their hunting.

Evan's graphic design and Seth's computer work kept them busy between road trips and paid their living expenses. Getting vengeance on murderous witches provided satisfaction, but it didn't cover the bills and often required expensive and arcane materials.

Their expenses were fairly minimal, aside from ammunition and arcane supplies, and they had been able to set aside a modest but growing nest egg. That cheered him on the nights he couldn't sleep, worried about surviving their quest.

"Hey, don't let your tacos get cold." Evan broke Seth out of his thoughts. The glint in Evan's eyes made it clear he suspected the direction Seth's musings had taken.

"Sorry. Did you try them? Any good?"

"They're great. I really like the mango salsa," Evan said, and Seth noticed that he had already polished off one of his three tacos.

"I'm glad. I was in the mood to cook something different."

"You keep me well fed," Evan replied with a sultry look that let Seth know his partner had more than food on his mind.

"Hold that thought," Seth teased, giving him a quick peck on the lips. "Let me clean up, and then we can have dessert." He reached over to stroke Evan's groin and felt him respond even through the denim.

They made quick work of the kitchen and headed to the living room since it was still too early for bed. The couch was roomy enough for both of them to fit, and Seth turned on a favorite music channel. Tonight, slow mutual hand jobs brought them to the edge and back several times before they came together, gasping for breath and glistening with sweat.

Seth cleaned them up with his discarded T-shirt. "Want to go again?"

Evan chuckled. "Tempting, but not tonight. That was…really good." He leaned in to give Seth a long, lingering kiss.

Seth clicked on a sci-fi movie they had both seen before, and they snuggled on the couch trading lazy kisses instead of paying attention.

"You're the best thing that ever happened to me." Seth held Evan close in his arms.

"I'd say the same about you—and not just because you saved my life," Evan teased.

"At this point, we've saved each other multiple times, so I think we've got that covered."

Evan gathered the discarded clothing and dishes while Seth made a final round to check locks and wards. They tumbled into bed together, and Seth felt the fatigue from being on high alert all day.

"Try not to think about the case. Get some sleep," he said in a low, fond voice as Evan rested his head on Seth's shoulder.

"You gonna do the same?" Evan kissed Seth's neck and reached over to push a lock of hair out of his eyes.

"I sure intend to try," Seth said. "We're no good to anyone if we're exhausted."

"Night. Love you." Evan sounded like he was already almost out.

"Love you too," Seth echoed. But despite his caution to Evan, his mind spun with loose ends and next steps until the wee hours.

The dream came after he finally fell asleep.

Seth found himself back at the side of the road where he and Jesse had gone legend tripping the night Jesse was murdered.

Jesse looked just as Seth remembered him, so young. But where Jesse's enthusiasm was a hallmark of his personality, tonight, he looked sorrowful.

"You didn't protect me. I trusted you, and you got me killed." Jesse's gaze felt like it bored right through Seth.

"I didn't know. Had no idea back then how to save you. I'm so, so sorry. I miss you so much."

"You're sorry. I'm dead. It's all your fault."

"Jesse—"

"You're going to get Evan killed too," Jesse went on, as sadness morphed into anger.

"I saved him. With what I learned after...we're getting vengeance on all of the witch-disciples. Taking revenge for what they did to you," Seth countered, feeling gut-punched by the accusations.

"Won't bring me back—and you got Mom and Dad killed too. It should have been you."

Seth blinked back tears. "Yes, it should have. I was the older brother. He took you by mistake. I would have gladly gone in your place if I could have made the choice."

"Evan would be safer without you. You destroy everyone who loves you."

"Jesse, please. Don't say that. Jesse—"

"Seth! Seth, wake up!" Evan's worried voice helped Seth shake off the last vestiges of sleep. He sat up in bed, heart pounding, drenched in sweat, with the fog of the dream in his mind and Jesse's voice ringing in his ears.

"You're safe. I'm safe. Whatever you dreamed, it's not real. We're okay," Evan told him.

Jesse's dead. That's real.

"What did you see?" Evan rubbed Seth's back and leaned close to him, solid and comforting. He pressed a kiss to Seth's shoulder.

Seth didn't want to divulge the awful accusations, but he and Evan had promised to be honest with each other. "I dreamed about Jesse. He blamed me for his death, for Mom and Dad," Seth replied in a choked voice just above a whisper. "He said I'd get you killed. That it should have been me instead of him. And he's right—I was the older brother."

"Seth Tanner, you listen to me," Evan said in a firm voice. "You saved my life, and we've saved so many of the intended victims. We're going to save Pax. Jesse didn't say those things; he told you himself that he loved you.

"That's your own guilt punishing you, but it's wrong. You didn't know back then. If you'd been the one who died, then I'd be dead now too, and so would all the other descendants, and there would be no end in sight. No one to stop the witch-disciples. Please, Seth. You've got to let this go."

Evan wrapped his arms around Seth, and Seth held on tight, biting back a sob as he buried his face in Evan's shoulder. Evan kept gently rubbing his back, kissing his neck, and murmuring reassurance until Seth no longer trembled and the awful dream receded.

"I'm here. We're together. And for tonight, we're safe," Evan repeated as they lay back down together. "Try to let it go. Tomorrow, we'll pick up the fight. Now, rest."

Seth didn't think it would be possible to fall asleep again, and he dreaded having the dream return, but sometime before dawn, his exhausted body gave in and sent him into a mercifully dreamless sleep.

"How are you this morning?" Evan walked into the kitchen after his shower. Seth had gotten up first, though well after dawn, got cleaned up, and started the coffee maker. Evan hugged him from behind and kissed the nape of his neck.

"Functioning," Seth replied. "I'm sorry about last night."

"Given what we do, it's pretty amazing we're as functional as we are," Evan replied. "Every now and then, we get overwhelmed. That's probably the most normal thing about our lives. It's okay. I'm here, I believe in you, and I've got your back."

Seth turned toward Evan and kissed him. "You're amazing. Thank you. Have a seat, the coffee is ready."

"Do you think that Vernon somehow sent that dream to fuck with your mind?" Evan asked.

Seth thought about it for a moment, then shook his head. "No. At least, he shouldn't have been able to with all our wards, protections, and charms. I'll check again, but we should be safe here. If it had been a vision when we were out and about, that would definitely be my first thought."

"Figured it was worth exploring. Still on to meet Kinsley?" Evan sat at the table.

Seth brought steaming cups of brew for both of them. "Yep. And I'm very interested to see what information she has and how she's willing to work with us."

SETH AND EVAN WERE OUTSIDE THE RESTAURANT EARLY, WAITING FOR Kinsley. Seth hadn't asked for a description, but he recognized her the moment a woman in her early thirties came into view. He sensed that she had power, although it was carefully hidden at the moment.

"Seth and Evan? I'm Kinsley." She had long dark hair and green eyes that, for just an instant, seemed to glow. They shook hands and went inside. Kinsley spoke a word to the person at the front podium, and a server escorted them to a private room in the back.

"We hold coven meetings here," she told them as they settled at a table, and the server returned with coffee. "I hope you don't mind, but to speed things along—and since I know the best stuff on the menu—I already ordered for us. Trust me, you won't be disappointed, and I guarantee you won't leave hungry."

Seth liked her already, and the nod he got from Evan let him know that his partner felt the same. Like Cassidy and her friends, Kinsley didn't act like her arcane abilities made her separate or different, although Seth already knew he would bet on her in a fight.

They ate first, a magnificent treat of raspberry-stuffed French toast with a generous dollop of whipped cream on top and a side of crispy bacon.

"You were right about the food." Seth dug in with gusto.

Evan shook his head fondly, although he ate with no less enthusi-asm. Even the bigger breakfasts they cooked on weekends in between cases didn't compare to the decadence of the restaurant's specialty.

"I know, right?" Kinsley said with a wink. "I love having an excuse to bring people here because I wouldn't dare come often and still fit into my clothing. All the other choices are almost as good. This one's my favorite."

"Good pick." Evan licked whipped cream off his lips. He didn't miss the heat that flashed in Seth's eyes at the sight.

When they were finished, the server topped off their coffee and left the pot.

"Rowan briefed me on the basics." Kinsley stirred sugar into her cup. "I've heard of Sterling Vernon and so has every witch in a hundred miles of Savannah. But all I know is that he's trouble. Dark magic practically oozes out of his pores if you have any psychic ability. He's got his hangers-on, but the covens and the more powerful witches stay out of his way."

"Has anyone ever gone up against him?" Seth wondered how Vernon kept his century-long lock on power.

"We don't go looking for trouble." Kinsley fixed him with a look. "He runs a restaurant, and he's got connections to a shipping company, but that doesn't interfere with coven priorities. He leaves other witches alone."

"What about the monsters that live in the city?" Evan looked up from his coffee. "Do the covens have any dealings with them?"

"You'll have to be more specific," Kinsley said. "Do you mean the politicians at City Hall or the supernatural beings?"

Evan raised an eyebrow. "Touché. I mean the paranormal creatures. Vampires, werewolves, succubi—the kind of beings that exist in every city under the radar."

"As long as the truces hold, we mostly ignore each other," Kinsley replied. "Rule Number One: don't call attention to magic and the para-normal. Rule Number Two: don't kill the mundanes. And Rule Number Three: don't leave bodies around that are going to break Rule Number One if you break Rule Number Two."

Seth wasn't surprised that the supernatural community was

divided, but it made it difficult to get the kind of insider information that would help uncover Vernon's weak spots.

"That doesn't mean there aren't individual exceptions," she added with a smirk. "I have a friend who is a vampire and another who is a necromancer. They're both relatively young, as those folks go, on their first normal lifespans. I trust them with my life, and so does the coven. I've already spoken with them, and they've got no love for Vernon. They're willing to help, for what it's worth."

"That could be worth quite a lot if push comes to shove," Evan replied. "Because someone is killing the cryptids and supernatural creatures that Vernon is serving for dinner at his secret restaurant. That means no one is safe."

Seth agreed, and technically Evan was right. But Seth had learned that supernatural creatures had their own pecking order and generally considered their own sort to be superior to all the others. Over the centuries, there had been alliances and betrayals, so which groups were currently friendly or at odds constantly shifted.

"I think you're right, but it could be a tough sell to convince the other groups that they're vulnerable. Especially if Vernon is only going after the beast-like cryptids that aren't human-based," Kinsley agreed. "There's still a lot of bias. Vernon would know how to play into that to keep himself and his enterprise safe."

"We don't know when Vernon is going to make his move against Pax, but it'll be soon, especially if he has an inkling that we're in town," Seth said.

"What's your next move?" she asked.

"Every witch-disciple has a protective amulet and an anchor for their magic. Together they provide protection and a well of power to draw on," Evan said. "We think Vernon's amulet is the necklace we've seen in several pictures. We're still trying to figure out the anchor, but our guess is that it may be an old ship's wheel. We need to find it and destroy it before we disrupt the ritual. It'll weaken him."

"Easier said than done," Kinsley replied.

"Seth and I think Vernon knows who we are, so we don't dare go to his regular restaurant, and we're too human to try to go to his monster joint," Seth replied. "We're going to ask a couple of local allies to go to his normal restaurant and see if they spot the anchor."

"I know we just met you, and this is a lot to ask, but do you think your vampire friend might be able to infiltrate the monster restaurant?" Evan asked. "Once we know where the anchor is, we can make plans to destroy it."

Kinsley took a moment to answer, and Evan considered it a win that she didn't refuse outright. "Maybe. It'll be up to him, of course. But I'll ask."

"Thank you," Seth replied, looking relieved.

"Vernon is vulnerable during the ritual. That's when we have to strike. If we can keep him from taking Pax, he's going to choose another sacrifice. It won't give him nearly as much of a boost as one of the original descendants of the deputies who killed Gremory, but without it, he's weaker and he knows it," Evan added.

"You're both descendants?" Kinsley seemed to be putting it all together.

"Yeah. My brother got killed instead of me," Seth replied. "And my father. Others too, farther back. Evan was the target for that disciple." He tried to keep his expression blank, ignoring memories of his nightmare.

"I lost family," Evan said. "This whole thing has gone on too long. So we're putting an end to it."

Kinsley's expression suggested that she also had felt the pain of losing someone to violence or dark magic. "I will do everything in my power to help you and rally helpers. I'm trusting you a lot on Rowan's say-so. Don't put my people in needless danger, or that protective magic will show you it has teeth."

"Understood," Seth replied, and Evan nodded.

Kinsley looked up as a young man with white-blond hair maneuvered through the tables to join them.

"This is Tristan," she told them. "My necromancer friend. Tristan, meet Seth and Evan, the hunters I told you about."

"Great to meet you." Tristan's boyish looks made Seth wonder how old the other man was, and guessed that he was probably in his midtwenties.

Seth glanced at Evan, wondering what his partner picked up from a necromancer in close proximity. Evan had a far-away look on his face, and Tristan turned to regard him thoughtfully, then nodded.

"You see them too," Tristan said.

"Yes, but not usually in the numbers that are gathered around you," Evan said. "That's quite an entourage."

Tristan laughed. "I've never thought of it like that, but I guess that's one way to look at it. The magic came to me very young, so I'm used to it." He paused. "I'm happy to help get this sleazebag out of Savannah. Just let Kinsley know when you need me, and I'll be there."

Seth and Evan left the restaurant after trading contact information and planned to check back the next day.

"That went pretty well," Evan said as they got into the truck.

"She didn't turn us into toads. He didn't call down the hordes of the dead. That's a plus."

Evan sighed and rolled his eyes. "We get a witch and her coven, plus a necromancer and maybe a vampire on our side. They might be able to check out the second restaurant. Beats going in alone."

"And we have Nash and Caden," Seth replied. "That's all important. But first, we've got to either get Pax out of danger or figure out how to protect him while shutting down Vernon."

"We've come up with something each time so far," Evan reminded him. "I believe in us."

Seth took his hand. "Good. Because I believe in us too."

They headed over to meet Nash at Mystic. Seth took a deep breath, enjoying the aroma of freshly brewed coffee.

"Come on in and get your caffeine fix," Nash told them, laughing. "My crew won't be in for another hour, and they don't need me for the prep anyhow. We won't be disturbed since we're not officially open."

They got cups of coffee and settled at a table in the back. The bar felt so different without the lights, music, and happy patrons, almost as if it was sleeping, or waiting to come back to life.

Nash lit the fat candle in the middle of the table and held his hands out to Seth and Evan. Seth watched Evan's face as they touched and saw him register an emotion he couldn't quite define.

"Spirits...hear us." Nash closed his eyes and took a deep breath.

Evan did the same, leaving Seth on guard to protect them physically, even if his options for magical defenses were more limited. "We need your wisdom and your help."

Seth felt the temperature drop. The barest hint of a breeze made the hair on his arms stand up, and he knew that the ghosts were present.

"Henry Miller. Paul Miller, if you can hear us, please draw near." Nash named Pax's father and grandfather. "Paxton is in danger from the same force that took your life. We're trying to protect him."

The air stirred again, this time enough to make the candle flame flicker. Evan's grip on Seth's hand grew tighter, and Seth knew from the look of deep concentration on his partner's face that some kind of connection was happening with the spirits.

"Paul?" Nash named Pax's grandfather. "Is that you?"

"Not an accident," Evan answered in a raspy voice that Seth almost didn't recognize. "Murdered."

"Did you know your killer?" Nash kept his eyes closed as he spoke.

"Not well. Recognized him," the ghost replied.

"Do you know his name?" Nash pressed.

"That Vernon guy," Paul's spirit said. "From downtown."

Seth hadn't been sure whether the two ghosts would have enough energy left to manifest after being drained for Vernon's ritual. *Then again, they've had years to recharge.*

Nash looked away as if someone had called his name. "Henry? Is that you?"

"I am Henry. It was Sterling Vernon. I tried to stop him." Nash's face went blank and his eyes glassy as the spirit answered his question.

"Where did you die?" Seth asked since both Evan and Nash had their full attention fixed on the ghosts.

"Don't know. Didn't see," Henry answered.

"Old factory," Paul's ghost said through Evan. "Paint."

Turpentine, Seth thought. *Like we suspected.*

"Protect Pax," Paul urged.

"How do we get him to believe us?" Seth asked.

"Tell him I said 'tugaloo,'" Henry's ghost replied. "He'll know."

"Stop Vernon," Paul's spirit pressed. "Save my grandson."

Both Nash and Evan shook off the connection with the ghosts as if waking from a doze. They both looked a bit confused.

"Did any of that happen out loud?" Evan looked to Seth for confirmation.

"Yes. I heard it all," Seth replied.

Nash looked equally befuddled, but he also nodded. "Paul and Henry were both here. I knew I was speaking for Henry, but it took my whole concentration."

"Henry was angry," Evan spoke up. "Maybe because he's more recently dead, but I got a strong sense of personality despite the ritual's toll. He's really worried about Pax."

"He said Pax would remember 'tugaloo,'" Seth said. "Does that make any sense to either of you?"

"It's a state park in South Carolina, near the Georgia border," Nash replied. "Maybe they went there as kids?"

"Let's hope Pax makes the connection." Evan took a gulp of his coffee like he was trying to clear away the last of the ghost's touch. "Of course, passing along a code word from a ghost isn't any less weird than telling him a witch is trying to kill him."

"Caden's been making some quiet inquiries about the old factory," Nash told them. "He's pretty sure Vernon's got some people inside the police department, so he doesn't want to tip our hand. Turns out there have been plenty of complaints about noise and bad smells coming from the turpentine plant since it shut down, but none of the reports indicated that the investigators found anything wrong."

"Convenient cover-up," Seth said.

"Which means bringing our own backup if that's where things go down," Nash pointed out. "Because we can't count on the cops."

Much as Seth hated dragging anyone else into danger confronting the witch-disciples, he had learned the hard way to accept help when it was offered, especially from friends with supernatural abilities.

"We've got a favor to ask." Evan then explained the need to find and destroy the anchor, their theory that it might be an old ship's wheel, and the possibility that it was part of the décor at Legacy.

"If we paid your tab, would you and Caden be willing to go there for dinner and see if you can pick up anything either from magic or the ghosts about whether the anchor is there?" Seth finished.

Nash chuckled. "Most people would jump at the chance for a free dinner for two there—it's pretty expensive. Although knowing Vernon's backstory, it's a little dicey. Let me talk to Caden, but I think we'll be up for it, assuming we can get a reservation."

"Thank you," Evan replied. "That would be a huge help."

"Let's hope we have time to pull the pieces together before Vernon makes his move," Seth said. "And cross your fingers that we can get Pax to listen. It would be nice to do this the easy way for once."

They thanked Nash and promised to return for dinner, then let him get back to preparing to open. Since it was nearly lunchtime, Seth headed back for the food truck lot and another opportunity to encounter Pax and Tony.

"You took all that pretty well in stride," Evan said as they looked for a parking space. "What did you make of it?"

Seth paused, weighing his words. He didn't envy Evan his ability with spirits, but he respected what his partner could do and the cost of his insight. "It always freaks me out a little when you're talking, but I know it's not really *you*," he admitted. "That's not a bad thing—I think your ability is amazing. But it makes me want to protect you. And a little...jealous? I don't like sharing you."

Evan chuckled. "If it helps, the ghost wasn't possessing me, just talking to me in my head so I can convey the message. Paul and Henry were pretty polite, as ghosts go. I don't have a splitting headache because they didn't push too hard."

"We've got confirmation of where Vernon's doing his dirty deeds," Seth said. "Straight from the victims. Now we've just got to outfox his particular brand of magic."

They parked and walked to the food trucks side by side, in sync as usual. Pax greeted them warmly when they reached the counter.

"What'll it be today, gentlemen? I'm glad you've found favorites here. You're going to miss us when you go home."

"Sticking with what works." Seth placed the same order they had before. "I imagine everyone tries to talk you into coming up with a way to ship your sauces from a website."

"Oh, if I had a dollar for every time that came up, I could buy a mansion," Pax agreed, ringing up their order as the workers behind him assembled the food. "There would definitely be an audience—but this right here is what I love about it, talking to people, meeting folks, and putting a good meal in your hands. Can't do that from a website."

They paid and thanked Pax, taking their orders to a table. Seth spotted Tony, but today the musician stayed with a pack of friends at a table close to the stage. Tony kept sneaking glances at them, and Seth wondered what lay behind Tony's sudden reticence after his earlier friendliness.

"Seem colder to you today than before?" Seth noticed that Evan's gaze had drifted to Tony as well.

"Yeah. Wonder what we did to look suspicious."

"We need to win over Tony to protect Pax." Seth dropped his voice so only Evan could hear him. "I'm hoping we get a chance to explain."

The food was just as good as before, impressing Seth with its consistency as well as the taste and quality. If they could keep Pax safe from Vernon, he had a bright future in Savannah's foodie community.

Someone else was on stage when they finished eating. Seth didn't see Tony when he and Evan got up to leave and wondered if the other man had left the area.

Instead, they found him waiting by their truck. "What's going on, and why are you hanging around Pax?" Tony challenged.

Seth had to give him credit for guts and loyalty. "Can't we just like the food?"

Tony glared. "I'd be more likely to believe that if the cameras at the house hadn't picked up this truck making several passes. It's definitely you—got a picture of the plate."

"Streets are public places. It's not a crime to drive on them." Seth wanted to figure out what Tony thought he knew before he tried explaining.

"We don't live on a through street," Tony said. "There's no reason for out-of-towners to be there, certainly not more than once."

Seth and Evan exchanged a look. "We're security consultants and we're here to protect Pax and you from the people who have been killing other men in his family."

Seth wondered how much Pax had told Tony about the deaths. Since their intel confirmed that the two men were a couple, Seth had assumed Tony knew that Pax had lost people close to him, even though Pax himself didn't know the true details.

Then again, not all relationships included sharing confidences, and Seth wasn't sure how long the two had been together or how serious they were.

Tony's eyes narrowed. "I don't know what you're talking about." It didn't require a psychic to tell that the musician's hackles had risen. He looked spooked.

"We're in Savannah to stop the cycle and keep Pax safe," Evan replied, meeting Tony's gaze.

Tony shook his head. "Cycle? What cycle? Pax said those deaths were accidents."

"They were made to *look* like accidents," Seth said in a level voice. "We're dealing with a serial killer who has latched onto Pax's family, and he believes that taking a sacrifice every dozen years will make him immortal."

Tony looked from Seth to Evan and back again. "Do you know how crazy that sounds?"

Less crazy than it will when we tell him Vernon is a dark witch with a coven and there's magic involved.

"Things can sound crazy and still be true," Evan replied.

"Are you guys FBI? Special Forces? CIA?"

"The same thing happened to my brother and father." Seth side-stepped the qualifications for now. "And it almost happened to Evan. He lost family, too. We intend to shut the problem down— permanently."

Tony's eyes widened. "Does that make you bounty hunters? Vigilantes? You sound like those guys on TV who hunt monsters."

Seth shrugged. "You're not far off the mark."

Tony took a step back. "That sounds illegal as fuck. Why not turn the killer over to the police if you've got the details?"

"It's complicated." Seth could see the skepticism in Tony's eyes and couldn't blame him. "We just want to protect you and Pax. Once it's over, you go back to your normal life like nothing happened and no worries, because the pattern of deaths is finished."

"You're crazy and dangerous," Tony said. "Leave us alone. Don't come around here again and stay the hell away from our house."

Seth held up a hand for a pause and took Caden's card from his pocket. "We'll keep our distance. His father's ghost said to tell Pax, 'Tugaloo.' Does that mean anything to you?"

He saw a flicker of recognition and uncertainty in Tony's eyes. "Maybe. You spoke to his father's *ghost?*"

"Our friend, a medium, talked to the ghosts of Henry and Paul Miller. They confirmed that they were murdered, and they worried that Pax would be next," Seth said.

"You're crazy," Tony countered. "This has to be some sort of scam."

Evan raised his hands, palms out, in appeasement. "We're the real deal. We're just trying to save Pax's life."

Seth handed over the business card. "I get that you don't trust us. But if something happens, call Detective Brady. Don't speak to anyone else except Caden. He's with the police, and he knows what's going on."

Tony looked at the card warily, but took it and slipped it into his pocket. "I mean it. Get lost. I'll take care of Pax."

Seth nodded. "I know you're going to try. But if things go wrong, you know who to contact."

He and Evan turned away, leaving Tony with a poleaxed expression.

"That went about as well as I expected," Evan muttered as they got into the truck.

"As I recall, you weren't quick to hop on board back then either." Seth started the engine and pulled away from the parking spot. "None of the targets have been. I can't blame them. Jesse and I were out that night legend tripping because we didn't believe either."

After all these years, the memory still flooded him with guilt. Evan laid a hand on his arm.

"We'll do everything we can to protect him, whether he and Pax believe or not. If we get rid of Vernon before he makes his move, maybe they never have proof. Doesn't matter. Their part of the curse will be broken," Evan replied.

"I don't know if Tony will tell him, but I hope the Tugaloo code-word gets Pax's attention."

By now it was time to drive to the conference center where Vernon was due to give his presentation. Seth and Evan had dressed in slightly better casual clothing so that they didn't stand out in a crowd, and Seth intended to stick to the farthest row from the stage where they could make a quick exit if necessary.

"Still want to go?" Evan asked as if he could read Seth's mind.

"We need to get a look at this guy, and this seems like our best bet without getting too close." Seth kept his eyes on the traffic.

They parked and headed inside. The unremarkable event space gave no clues about Vernon's other life, and the other attendees who gathered in the atrium, waiting to be let into the auditorium, were dressed in relaxed business attire. If any belonged to Vernon's coven, they hid it well.

A banner advertising Vernon as the guest speaker listed him as "Owner, Legacy Restaurant" among other awards and kudos but didn't have a photo. Instead, the ship's wheel logo figured promi-nently in the design.

Seth glanced to Evan, a silent question about ghosts that his partner picked up on right away. Evan shook his head. So far, the program appeared to be exactly as advertised—a presentation on increasing restaurant profitability in a changing marketplace.

They slid into seats at the end of the top row, where the dim lighting might hide their faces and the nearby door offered a quick exit. The people seated nearby chatted in low voices about completely mundane topics like the best location to get lattes and what they planned to cook for dinner.

A man in a dark suit strode onto the stage, and the audience stirred. "Ladies and Gentlemen, welcome to the latest edition of our Afternoon Business Briefings series," he said. "We're glad you're here, and on behalf of the Savannah Chamber of Commerce and our city's Restau-rant Association and Small Business Council, we hope today's presen-tation provides helpful insights as well as food for thought.

"And now, I present veteran restaurateur and area philanthropist, Sterling Vernon!"

The crowd clapped enthusiastically. The age stated in Vernon's bio listed him as fifty-three, although thanks to the magic, he was a century older. He cut a handsome figure with enough gray hair to look distinguished and wore an expensive suit with tailoring that flattered his stocky form.

Vernon waved to the crowd with a broad smile. "Thank you, everyone, for that wonderful welcome. And thank you for coming out for this presentation. I hope you'll find it useful, and I wish you all continued business success."

Seth felt the moment Vernon's gaze landed on them. For just a few seconds, as he adjusted his microphone, the man hesitated, as if thrown off script. He recovered quickly, and while his smile and easy manner never failed, his stare bored into Seth and Evan with malevolent intensity.

Vernon's speech captivated the audience with a polished but folksy mixture of personal stories about challenges faced and overcome in restaurant settings along with motivational patter to encourage other owners to continue to chase their dream. Seth wondered whether Vernon used any magic to keep his audience so engaged with what seemed to him to be commonplace advice.

When the audience stood for a final ovation, Seth plucked at Evan's sleeve, and they slipped out using the wall of bodies as a screen to avoid Vernon's notice. Two burly men in dark suits milled around the lobby, presumably bodyguards.

They made a beeline for Seth and Evan.

Seth glanced to Evan to make sure he saw the danger, then led them into the crowd of attendees leaving the auditorium where the goons would be too visible making a move.

As soon as they could, Seth ducked out a side door with Evan on his heels.

The two henchmen lunged at them. Seth dodged and returned a roundhouse kick, sending his attacker sprawling. The second man grabbed Evan by the shirt-front and punched him in the side before Evan boxed his ears and landed a kick to the knee. Evan's protective amulet fell to the ground, pulled loose by the attack. He scooped it up and ran with Seth right beside him.

"We haven't lost them," Evan said as they picked up speed once they reached the sidewalk.

"Stay close." Seth veered off the sidewalk into traffic, dodging between cars to reach the other side. The light changed, making it harder for the goons to follow.

The men kept up their pursuit. Seth led them away from the truck but wondered how far the guards would go to follow them. He spotted a city bus pulling up to a stop with a line of waiting passengers and ran for it. The door closed on Evan's heels, and the bus pulled away, leaving their pursuers stewing angrily on the sidewalk.

"Any idea where this bus goes?" Evan fixed the clasp on his amulet and dropped it back around his neck.

"Doesn't matter," Seth replied. "We'll ride a couple of stops, get out, and walk back a different, not-logical route. Those guys can't watch every street."

Seth half expected the men to get on the bus at the next stop, but perhaps the reality of an audience and security cameras kept them from following. When no one suspicious got on after the next two stops, Seth and Evan paid their toll and got off, then used GPS to take a circuitous route back to where they parked.

Seth didn't realize he had been holding his breath until they got into the truck.

"Wait," he said as Evan reached for the door handle. "Something's wrong. I'm picking up a jangle of bad magic. Check to make sure those assholes didn't plant anything on us."

Seth didn't find anything on himself, but Evan froze as he put his hand into his jacket pocket and withdrew it like he had been burned. "There's something in here I didn't have before."

Seth tried to look calm despite a spike of panic. "Okay, don't touch it. I've got a binding box in the back of the truck. It'll contain the magic. Then we'll call Kinsley or Rowan for help."

Thinking back, the goons' attack hadn't been as dangerous as he would have expected. *Maybe it was a distraction, and the real attack is whatever they planted on Evan.*

Seth pulled out the warded iron box and opened the lid. Evan peeled off his jacket and placed it inside. A small, crudely carved wooden figure fell out of a pocket. Seth slammed the lid shut.

"Was that some kind of voodoo doll?" Evan asked. "It looked like the sort of thing sailors whittle to pass the time."

Fuck, fuck, fuck, Seth thought, trying to stay calm for Evan's sake. He grabbed Evan's arm and steered him back toward the truck door. "We'll figure it out. Let's go before they come back." Seth hoped he sounded calmer than he felt.

Seth barely kept himself from screeching away from the curb. "Vernon had to have sent them after us. Either he had already told them what we looked like before the presentation, or he got word to them when he saw us there."

"My vote is before. They didn't spot us going in or couldn't nab us without causing a scene," Evan replied. "Lucky for us, Savannah has a good bus system."

"What did you make of the presentation?" Seth asked after they drove for a few minutes. His mind raced thinking of the magical item the goon had planted on Evan, but for the moment, his partner seemed okay.

Evan looked thoughtful. "Honestly? I thought he was boring. I could find a dozen better speeches on YouTube. He didn't say anything very original, and he certainly didn't acknowledge that when you've got a century of experience and wealth behind you, success is easier."

Seth couldn't help laughing. "True. Although I thought he looked good for his age."

Evan rolled his eyes. "Human sacrifice will do that, I guess. And did you see the ship's wheel logo on the banner? My money is still on the original as his anchor." He was silent for a few moments. "Maybe it was a mistake to go to the event."

Seth shook his head. "No. Seeing us rattled him." *Although I'm worried about that thing they planted in your pocket.*

"If he's planning to sacrifice Pax soon, he shouldn't be surprised that we're on his tail given what happened with the other disciples. He just might not have thought we had the balls to show up at his event," Seth added.

"Now what?" Evan seemed nervous.

Seth reached over and took his hand. "Hey. We've destroyed more than half of those witchy bastards. We'll get Vernon too and save Pax."

"I wish we had a more solid plan."

"Yeah, well it's always a bit mushy in the middle waiting for an opening. But we've got Caden and Nash on our side, plus Kinsley, her coven, Tristan, and her friend the vampire. Teag and Rowan could be here from Charleston in less than three hours if we need them. That's a lot more help than we had with some of the first disciples," Seth reminded him.

He agreed with Evan, wishing they could create a playbook in advance to rely less on luck and more on strategy, but experience had shown them that the situation remained extremely fluid, sometimes until the very last moments. His military experience helped a lot, but it didn't cover magic.

"I can't help feeling like I'm waiting for the other shoe to drop," Evan confessed. "He couldn't exactly hit us with lightning bolts in front of that whole audience, but that doesn't mean he won't do something later."

"You're the one with the intuition," Seth said. "Is there anything specific that's got you worried?"

Evan let out a long breath. "No. Just a feeling of foreboding. I know we're doing good work hunting the disciples, and if you hadn't started the quest, I'd be dead. But I'll be glad when it's over."

"Me, too."

They called ahead and picked up takeout for dinner before heading back to the RV, not wanting to be out in public more than necessary. The restaurant was one that Caden had recommended. Dinner was Brunswick stew with freshly baked bread, accompanied by fried green tomatoes topped with a house-made pimento cheese spread.

Evan rubbed his temples.

Seth frowned. "Headache?"

"Yeah. Came on kinda suddenly," Evan replied. "It seems a little better now that we're home. I'm not going to let it spoil a great meal. The food smells fantastic."

"Do you feel okay otherwise?" Everything going on was certainly enough to give anyone a migraine.

"I'll be okay."

"I've got good whiskey," Seth said with a smile. "Maybe it will help."

They did their best not to talk about the case as they ate, seizing a few moments of reprieve. The food was as good as it smelled, another confirmation of the city's reputation as a great place to eat.

After supper, Seth found an action movie online that they hadn't seen, and they settled in with a bowl of popcorn to extend the short break from their case. He could see Evan close his eyes now and then against the headache, but every time Seth asked, Evan waved off his concern.

Several hours after dinner, Seth's phone rang from a number he didn't recognize. He handed it to Evan, who put it on speaker.

"Seth? Seth, is that you? Caden gave me your number."

It took Seth a moment to recognize Tony's panicked voice. He exchanged a worried look with Evan.

"Tony, what's wrong?" Evan asked.

Seth noticed he was rubbing his temples again, and his pinched expression suggested that the headache was worse.

"Pax is gone. He didn't leave on his own. I know he wouldn't. Everything is still here, just no Pax," Tony said all in one breath.

"Slow down," Seth coached. "Tell us what happened."

Tony was quiet for a moment. Seth could hear his panicked breathing gradually slow.

"The day at the truck was normal. Creepy guy didn't even show up. Business was good, lots of regulars and some new tourists. We closed on time and stopped at the grocery store on the way home for some stuff to cook dinner," Tony said.

"I'm sorry I was rude earlier. I was...scared. But I took what you said seriously, and I kept a lookout for anything suspicious. I swear I didn't see anything odd." Tony sounded young and frightened.

"We believe you," Evan encouraged. "What happened after the grocery store?"

"I took a load into the house, and Pax was supposed to be right behind me," Tony answered. "Except he wasn't. Between the car and the house, he vanished. The bag was on the ground, but no Pax. I called for him, but he didn't answer. There was no one in sight. No cars driving away, nothing." Tony's voice held unshed tears, and Seth didn't fault him for the reaction.

"I told Detective Brady—Caden—everything, and he said that he would come out. I didn't expect him to visit personally, but he came with Nash from the pub, and they did some police stuff and some other tests I'd never seen before. Spooky stuff."

"What did they say?" Evan asked.

"Nash said that he believes Pax is still alive because he couldn't find a ghost." He choked back a sob. "Caden touched the grocery bags that Pax dropped and closed his eyes, and told us that a man said words that made Pax pass out, and that he and another man kidnapped him. He reported Pax as a possible kidnapping victim and gave the details about the car, but...I don't think someone took him for his wallet."

Seth closed his eyes as old memories welled up. "No. It wasn't a robbery. The people who took him were likely witches who could keep from being noticed."

"That's what Caden said when he was done talking to the other cops," Tony said. "This is all my fault. I should have listened to you—"

"No, it isn't," Evan said in a stern tone. "What we told you was difficult to believe—impossible under normal circumstances. You were right to be wary. We knew Vernon was going to move on him soon, but we didn't know when."

"If I had listened to you, maybe you could have put him some-where safe. Is there a magical witness protection program?" Tony asked. "I would have made him believe me. Now—"

"Tony, listen to me. There's no guarantee that we could have gotten to Pax before they did. They used magic to take him, and they could have used that against us too. The bad guy was closer to making his move than we thought. As for a witness protection program...sort of. I'm not sure we could have gotten him there with the witch on our tail."

Evan knew that Seth meant the St. Expeditus Society in Charleston, which gave sanctuary to people hunted by supernatural criminals.

"Where are you?" Evan asked.

"At home." He gave a shaky laugh. "I haven't even put the groceries away."

Seth and Evan traded a look, and Evan nodded. "We'll come get you. Stick the perishables in the fridge. You can stay with us. We don't have a lot of elbow room, but the RV is heavily protected, and we picked up enough dinner to share. Don't go anywhere, lock the doors, and ignore anyone who knocks except for us. We'll be there as quickly as we can."

"Okay. Thank you. Just...hurry." Tony sounded like he was barely holding himself together.

"Stay on the line. Talk to me. About anything," Evan said as he and Seth locked the RV, climbed into the truck, and headed back to town. "Tell me how you got into music?"

"My grandfather used to play the guitar. He taught me. He was with a bunch of local bands when he was young," Tony said, shaky but distracted. "He didn't care that I was gay. Said he'd played with plenty of gay guys in the bands and it never bothered him. The rest of the family, not so much," he added with a bitter sigh.

"How'd you end up in Savannah? Where else do you play besides the food truck park and Mystic?" Evan did his best to keep Tony engaged.

"I left home and headed to the big city, which was Savannah. Told myself I'd work up to Atlanta, but it's got a real different energy. Wasn't ready for that. Maybe never will be. Savannah's been good to me," Tony said. "I found people to play with who aren't jerks, so sometimes I play alone, and sometimes we have a trio. We have regular gigs lined up that pay enough to cover the rent. And I met Pax."

"How did you meet?" Evan looked over to Seth, who mouthed, "Five more minutes."

"I was playing at a bar, and he came in with some friends from the food trucks," Tony said. "They hung around and seemed to be really into the music. Then his friends left, and Pax stuck around for my second set. He bought me a beer afterward and we got talking. Everything else just grew from there. How did you and Seth meet?"

Evan rolled his eyes. "Seth told me that a dark witch wanted to kill me. I said he was crazy. Then it turned out he was right, and he saved my life. It sounds very made-for-TV dramatic, but I'd definitely recommend the way you and Pax met."

Seth pulled up in front of the house Tony and Pax shared. He and Evan both drew their guns, although they kept them low to avoid drawing the wrong sort of attention.

"I don't see anyone," Evan said.

"A witch with a cloaking spell might be able to hide," Seth warned.

"I'm not getting any warnings from the ghosts," Evan replied. "They saw Pax get taken, and the ones who still have a sense of self are worried about Tony."

"Will they stand watch while we get Tony out of there?" Seth asked.

Evan closed his eyes, concentrating, and then nodded. "Yeah. But I don't think they can fight if we get ambushed."

"Then we better not need backup," Seth replied.

Tony was waiting inside the door with a packed duffel bag and his guitar. He looked like he had been crying, although he now wore a resolute expression.

"I don't know anything about how you guys do what you do, but I'll help any way I can to take those bastards down and get Pax back." Tony locked the door behind him, and they hustled him into the truck.

"Stay down," Seth told him as they drove away. "Just in case anyone is watching."

Tony tucked himself into the footwell in the back seat where he couldn't be seen from the windows as Seth put them back on the road.

"Is anyone following us?" Tony asked in a shaky voice.

"Not that I can tell," Seth replied. "I'm going to take the long way, just in case."

Seth made several switchbacks and meandering turns before finally ending up at the RV park.

"Stay put," he told Tony as he got out to check the wards on the trailer and scope out the area before gesturing for Tony and Evan to come inside.

"This is where you guys live?" Tony asked, looking around the neat, compact living space.

"It's cozy, but it's home," Evan said.

"My folks bought it to do some retirement sightseeing before they were killed by the witch-disciple who also killed my brother," Seth replied.

"That's terrible. I'm so sorry," Tony said.

"It's what put all the rest of this in motion," Seth told him. "Go ahead and set your duffel down by the couch. It has a pull-out bed. I'm afraid that's all we can offer for sleeping, but I've got sheets, extra pillows, and blankets to make it comfortable."

Tony tucked his bag into a corner and then came to sit at the kitchen table. "Thank you for letting me come with you. I didn't know what to do."

Evan got the takeout order from the fridge and set it on the counter. "You're welcome to share what we brought home. If you prefer a sandwich, I've got ham and turkey, two kinds of cheese, condiments, and pickles. What sounds good? Food always helps."

"Ham. Any kind of cheese. Thanks," Tony replied, sounding dazed.

Evan made a sandwich, grabbed a bag of chips and a can of soda, then he put the plate in front of Tony before he grabbed a folding chair, and Seth sat across from him with their own plates of takeout. No one talked for a few minutes. Seth figured they were all trying to recalibrate after everything that had happened.

Tony ate, although it didn't look like he had much appetite. Seth couldn't blame him, given his worry for Pax. When Tony finished, Evan picked up the plate and put it in the dishwasher, then joined the others in the living room.

"You drink whiskey?" Seth asked.

"Huh? Yeah." Tony sat on the couch with his head in his hands. Seth poured them all a couple of fingers' worth in mismatched glasses, enough to ease the stress without taking away their fighting edge.

Tony accepted his glass gratefully and knocked it back, then sputtered.

"Go easy." Evan sipped from his glass.

Seth wondered if Evan's sudden headache had gone away and guessed from the look in his eyes that it hadn't. That worried him.

"I'm scared," Tony admitted. "I'm afraid that they'll hurt Pax, and I'm ashamed that I didn't stop them. I'm terrified for him—he's got to be so afraid. And I don't know how I can help you get him back."

Seth and Evan sat down in the other chairs. "Evan and I went to Sterling Vernon's award ceremony today. Does that name ring a bell?"

Tony frowned. "The restaurant guy? He did a mentorship program for up-and-coming owners, and Pax went to it. Pax said Vernon was really nice to him and very helpful, but I've always gotten an uncomfortable feeling around him. Why?"

"Because he's really a century-old witch who was behind all the deaths in Pax's family, and he's the one who arranged the kidnapping." Once again, Seth wondered if Tony had some latent, unrecognized psychic ability.

Tony blinked, looking stunned. "What? How?"

Seth figured that ripping the band-aid off was the only way to bring Tony up to speed. "A century ago, a dark witch named Rhyfel Gremory had a coven of twelve witch-disciples. He sacrificed people to work an immortality spell for himself and his coven. When he was hunted down and killed for his crimes, his followers scattered, claiming their own territories and setting up covens to work the spell to their benefit. They require a cycle of human sacrifice to make the magic work. It doesn't end until the disciple is dead."

"That's...pretty crazy." Tony looked at his glass like he was sorry he had drunk the liquor so quickly. Seth poured about half as much into the glass.

"Go slow. We don't have time to nurse a hangover," Seth advised.

"If you...stop...Vernon," Tony said, as if he couldn't quite bring himself to say "kill", "what about the rest of his coven? Do you have to stop them too?"

Evan shook his head. "It depends. If the rescue comes in the middle of the ritual once the magic is activated, the repercussions destroy the witch-disciple and his coven. If we can stop Vernon before he starts the ritual, the rest may scatter, trying to cover their asses."

"I don't understand what Vernon gets out of it." Tony looked very lost. "He's already rich and well-known. He's a big player in the local scene. Does he really plan to live forever?"

Evan shrugged. "It's extended his life to more than a century without normal aging. And he's been bankrolling his restaurant with smuggling and other illegal activities. He's got an underground restaurant that caters to a supernatural clientele with some highly illegal menu items."

Tony swallowed hard. "Bad stuff?"

"You probably don't want to know," Evan replied.

"Okay. How can I help you save Pax?" Tony asked. His eyes were red-rimmed, but his resolute gaze told them he wouldn't be dissuaded.

"I don't know yet," Seth said. "I'm going to put out the call to our friends with abilities that Pax has been taken. We're sure we know where Vernon's hiding him. Once they get here, we can go in to save Pax and shut down Vernon's killing spree for good."

"What's stopping his goons from coming after us here?" Tony asked.

Seth sat back. "Magic. I'm not a full witch, but I can do some protective spells that our more powerful friends developed. They've shown us how to put wards on the truck and RV and given us protective charms."

He dug in his pocket and pulled out a talisman Rowan had given him. "Here. Put this on. It won't make you completely magic-proof, but it will help."

Tony looked at the charm with a skeptical expression, then placed the chain around his neck. "Now what?"

"Now Evan and I start calling in the troops and pulling what we need together to go after Pax," Seth replied. "For the moment, you should rest. I promise we'll find ways for you to help. But I'm not going to put you in unnecessary danger. Pax would never forgive us if we lost you to get him back."

Tony looked away and sniffed, swiping at his eyes with the back of his hand. "I'm not hero material, but I'll do whatever I can to help you bring him home safely. He means everything to me."

Evan gave him an encouraging smile. "We understand. And we're going to move heaven and hell to bring him back safely and make sure this doesn't happen to anyone else."

Evan got Tony settled on the couch and brought a stack of bed linens for later. Once Tony was comfortable with more whiskey and a movie on one of the streaming channels, Seth and Evan sat at the table with a fresh pot of coffee.

"How's your headache?" Seth gave Evan an appraising look.

Evan grimaced. "Still there. It seemed better when we first got back to the RV, but it's gotten worse. Probably stress."

Seth gave him a worried once-over, thinking that Evan looked pale, and guessing from the tension around his eyes that the headache hurt more than his partner let on.

"Here." Seth dug out one of the extra amulets. "Just in case yours got damaged when that jerk pulled it off." Evan accepted the necklace and slipped it over his head, on top of the original one. By unspoken agreement, they left the magical lock box and the whittled figure in the truck.

"That...helps," Evan said. Seth's heart sank, and he saw understanding in Evan's eyes.

"That carved thing they put in my pocket—it whammied me, didn't it?" Evan asked with fear in his voice.

"That was no accident. He pulled off your amulet and then slipped you the carving," Seth growled.

"Do you think Rowan or Kinsley can lift the spell?" Evan asked.

"I'm sure as hell gonna find out." Seth had silenced his phone and computer to avoid disrupting their heart-to-heart with Tony, but both devices had been reporting new messages almost constantly since he had put out the alarm.

"Rowan and Teag will be here first thing in the morning." Seth skimmed his notices. "Kinsley says her coven and her friend the necromancer are in on taking down Vernon, and they're gathering at her place, setting up the materials they need for when it's time to move." His thumbs flew across the buttons, tapping out a terse summary of the problem and asking for help.

"Nash and Caden had their dinner at Legacy," Seth reported as they waited to hear back from the two witches. "They didn't pick up on anything there that seemed like the anchor, but he's tapping into the ghosts to see what more we can learn about Vernon's monster restaurant. Caden can't officially do more than report Pax as a missing person, but *unofficially* he's bringing some bodyguard-types he trusts for armed backup who won't freak out over the woo-woo."

"And?" Evan's voice remained steady even though he looked pale and worried.

"We could use a central command center." Seth weighed his words as he thought through the possibilities. "Someone who is in communication with everyone that we can reach if anything goes south. Who has backup contacts in case we need to call in the cavalry, meaning the rest of Cassidy's friends. Tony could stay here and be safe and still be an enormous help."

"I think that sounds—"

Evan's eyes fluttered, and the color drained from his face. He grabbed the edge of the table to steady himself and looked like he might pass out.

"Evan? What's wrong?"

"Everything," he said thickly. "Whatever I've got, it's worse."

Seth took Evan's hand. "We'll figure it out. I promise."

Seth's phone rang. "Rowan? Thank God. I'm going to put you on speaker."

"Seth, Evan. I've got Kinsley with me. Now what's all this about curses?"

Seth gave the two witches a recap and described the carved totem as clearly as he could after just a brief view. "Evan actually touched it before we knew what had happened. I didn't touch the carving, but I did move his jacket with it in the pocket, and that doesn't seem to have affected me. It's in our lockbox in the truck right now."

They heard a muffled buzz of voices as the two women conferred. Seth wondered if Rowan had put her hand over the phone for a moment of private discussion.

"Tell us how Evan's faring," Kinsley said. "What are the symptoms?"

"I feel like my head is going to explode," Evan replied. "I think I'm getting a fever. Achy all over. But I felt totally fine before I touched that damn carving."

"Can you tell us anything more about the carving?" Rowan asked.

"We did our best not to handle it," Seth replied. "But if you need me to, I can go back out to the truck and use iron tongs to get a better look."

"I don't think that will be necessary," Rowan said quickly. "Just tell us what you remember."

Seth and Evan chimed in with their impressions from the short glimpse before they slammed the lockbox closed. "It was crudely carved, not as good as what someone who really is good at whittling can do," Seth said.

"It reminded me of a single figure with a roughed-in face and not very many details," Evan agreed. "Wooden. There might have been a splash of red or orange on it, but not like someone tried to paint it carefully."

They heard muffled conversation once more, then Rowan came back on the line. "There's a long history of using carved figures for hexing and blessing. Giving a blessed figure to someone who was already ill could heal them. Giving a cursed one conveys the curse."

"What can we do to break it?" Seth looked at Evan and his heart hurt.

"Considering the situation, I'd bet that this was Vernon's way of throwing down the gauntlet," Kinsley replied. "You've already done all the normal things to make it better: put it in a lockbox made to contain magical items, taken Evan inside a warded space with salt rings, and used protective charms. That's slowing down the curse, but it isn't enough to stop it."

"Should I burn the figure?"

"No!" Both Rowan and Kinsley spoke at once. "At least, not until we're sure."

"Then what?" Seth asked.

Evan met his gaze. "I think Vernon's challenged you to a duel to the death. His or mine."

Seth caught his breath. He'd considered that possibility when Kinsley used the word "gauntlet," but quickly cast it aside.

"I think Evan's right," Rowan replied.

"So do I, unfortunately," Kinsley concurred. "You haven't been in town long enough for him to have time to do much unless he was expecting you sooner or later. That's my bet. You showed up, he recognized you, and already had a plan."

"What can we do?" Seth felt completely adrift. *We shouldn't have gone to that presentation. Practically served ourselves up on a platter.*

Evan gave him a look as if he could guess Seth's thoughts. "Stop beating yourself up. If he was expecting us, he would have found a pretext one way or the other. Don't forget, those two guys came at us around the food trucks, so they already knew about us. If the attack hadn't been the seminar, it could have been while we were getting gas or buying dinner."

"Evan's right," Rowan said. "But just because he got the jump on you doesn't mean he's won the game. Work your plan. When you destroy Vernon, it will break the curse, and Evan should be safe." She paused. "I'll stop by and see if there's anything else I can do to at least make him comfortable."

"Okay." Seth felt a little breathless and still had a tight grip on Evan's hand. "Thank you. Is everyone ready for tomorrow?"

"We've got a good team and a solid plan," Rowan told him. "You've defeated the rest of the witch-disciples you've fought. You can nail this guy too."

But it's always been me and Evan working together since that first time.

Evan gave his hand a squeeze. "I'll still be helping. Just from here instead of there. We can do this. I believe in us."

"Thanks," Seth told the witches. "Then we stick to the timeline. See you then." The call ended, and he took a deep breath, trying to steady his nerves.

Sterling Vernon made his move. And I've got to respond, or Evan dies.

4

EVAN

"SETH?"

Seth stared at the phone like it might bite. He looked like he was fighting down panic and paused to take a deep breath before he replied. He held Evan's hand in both of his. "I'm going to fix this. I swear by all that's holy, I'm not going to let that curse take you."

Evan realized he had begun hyperventilating.

"Breathe. It's not over until it's over, and I'm going to get that son of a bitch." Seth's voice was strong and comforting.

"He'll be waiting for us. This is his way of forcing us to walk into a trap. You can't do that."

"The hell I can't!" Seth's outburst made Evan jump and attracted Tony's notice. "Vernon knew we were after Gremory's disciples. The only question was which of them we'd go for next. He's already been on notice that we were coming for him, sooner or later."

"When we went to the presentation—" Evan felt guilty about tipping their hand.

Seth shook his head. "No. He realized we were in town before that. Remember, he had someone watching Pax. Then those goons jumped us at the truck."

"If he knew you were coming, why did he wait to take Pax? Why not take him before you got here?" Tony had left the couch and came to stand behind Evan's chair.

"From what we've learned, the ritual raises the most power when it's done at the right time. Otherwise, it doesn't recharge the witch-disciple's magical battery as much. So there's an incentive to stick to the schedule. Vernon was watching Pax, so I don't think we've changed his plans much."

Evan knew Seth well enough by now to spot the disconnect between his voice and his eyes. Seth's tone remained calm and controlled, but the desperate look in his eyes told another story.

Evan gripped Seth's hand firmly. "Don't count me out yet. I'm not planning on going anywhere for a long, long time. Vernon changed the timing, but it was always going to be a fight to the death, us against him. Just like it's been with every one of the disciples."

A wave of vertigo washed over Evan, and he swayed in his chair. Tony put a hand on his shoulder to steady him.

"You're going to need to sit this one out," Seth told Evan. "He's got his claws into you."

"I'm not just going to lie around while the rest of you fight the battle," Evan snapped.

"Um, excuse me," Tony put in. "Didn't you just say that you wanted a central command center? Maybe now you have one." He looked from Seth to Evan. "You want me to stay here, inside the wards. I wouldn't know how to coordinate your information and allies, but Evan does. We'll stay together. He can tell me what to do, and I can take care of him and do anything he can't."

"That makes a lot of sense." Seth looked at Evan. "What do you think? You'll still be in the game, being backup, using the ghosts for intel and surveillance. Both of you will be safe, and Tony can help if you feel worse."

Evan hated the idea of not being right behind Seth heading into the fight, but he couldn't deny that he felt too sick to hold his own. *I'd be a liability, and while Seth was worrying about me, Vernon could get lucky.*

"I know how to shoot a gun." They both looked at Tony. "My grandpa taught me. I brought my Glock; it's in my bag. I go to the shooting range now and again to keep sharp." He sighed. "I never told Pax. He's uncomfortable with weapons, but I wasn't going to let anyone threaten us without a fight."

"Kinsley has a friend who's a necromancer," Seth said. "Ghosts always end up playing an important part, and if Evan isn't there and Nash is leading the charge at the monster meat location, maybe Tristan can help."

"Okay, we'll man the phone lines," Evan capitulated. "But you'd damn well better come back to me." He held Seth's hand hard enough to make his partner wince. "Do not sacrifice yourself to save me, do you understand? This only ends one way: with you, me, Tony, and Pax alive. Got that?"

Seth nodded, and Evan released his hold. "I promise. We were all going to be in mortal danger even without the curse. Vernon just put a different spin on it."

Seth dialed Kinsley and put her on speaker phone. She picked up on the third ring. "Hey, it's Seth. Is Tristan still available and willing to help us out?"

"I will ask, but I think he's counting on it," Kinsley replied. "I can call him back with details."

Seth let out a breath. "Yes, please. Without Evan or Nash at the turpentine plant fight, I'm afraid we'll be at a real disadvantage."

"I'll call him right now and let you know what he says," Kinsley promised. "Be back to you soon." She ended the call.

Seth reached for his cup and downed the last of his long-cold coffee. "I'll feel better if that works out," he told Evan and Tony. "We need to let the rest of the crew know the plan. There's not going to be a chance to catch Vernon completely by surprise since we have to strike when he starts the ritual, but Kinsley and Rowan might see times that are better for us than others."

"I can at least help make phone calls." Evan set his jaw. "Let's figure out what we're saying, so we're both on the same page."

Either Seth didn't feel like arguing or he decided that giving ground on this issue wouldn't cause harm, because he grabbed a pen and paper and wrote several lines before sliding the call script over to Evan.

It read: "Vernon cursed Evan to force a confrontation. He has to stick to a schedule for the ritual, but he might have some wiggle room. How fast can you be ready?"

Evan nodded. "Works for me. Tell me who you want to call, and I'll contact the others."

"Since it looks like we're going to be up for a while, how about I make a snack?" Tony said. "An army runs on its stomach."

"That would be great," Seth said, and Evan nodded enthusiastically even though the curse had his stomach in knots. He reminded himself that Tony was putting on a brave face after Pax's disappearance, and giving him a way to be busy and useful was a kindness.

"Thank you," Evan added.

"Mind if I raid your pantry?" Tony eyed the kitchen cabinets.

"Go for it," Seth told him. "We just stocked up before we came to town, so there should be plenty to pick from."

"What about the time to meet?" Evan asked.

"I hate to say it, but I think dawn is our best bet," Seth replied. "Sunrise has its own supernatural energy, so that could help us. There's less likelihood of mundane interference. And if tomorrow is the date Vernon intended, then he may have leeway for when he begins. He may not expect us at such an inconvenient time."

With the script and dividing up the phone numbers, the calls went quickly. All of their friends were aghast at Vernon's escalation, but said they could be ready to go at dawn at the old turpentine factory.

Kinsley called back about half an hour later. "Tristan is in. I also talked to my vampire friend who went to that monster meat restaurant. He stayed at the bar so he didn't have to eat the food, but he confirmed that the place's customers were a mixed bunch of supernatural creatures who looked human. And that ship's wheel you were looking for, there was a big one on the wall that looked old."

"Thank you," Evan told her. "And thank your friend for us, please."

"Glad to help. Tristan and I will be there tomorrow."

Evan put down his phone when he finished the last call, waiting for Seth to wrap up his conversation. In the kitchen, Tony whistled quietly as he took cookie sheets out of the oven.

"I don't know what you made, but it smells fantastic," Evan told Tony.

Tony beamed. "I'm not the chef Pax is, but I can make a mean batch of sheet pan nachos. They'll be ready to eat as soon as they cool down."

Seth's phone rang. Evan recognized Nash's number when it popped up on the screen.

"Sorry about the whole curse thing," Nash said when Seth accepted the call, since they had already phoned him and Caden to confirm the next day's plan.

"I've got confirmation that Vernon's anchor is at the monster meat restaurant. Any thoughts on how we steal the wheel and destroy it?" Seth asked.

"I have an idea about that," Nash replied. "It's a little illegal."

Seth barked a laugh. "Everything we'll be doing tomorrow is at least a little illegal. What's your idea?"

Nash cleared his throat. Evan wondered if the other man looked around to make sure his cop partner wasn't in earshot. "The monster restaurant is in what appears to be an abandoned diner. It sits off by itself in a run-down part of town that went downhill when the roads changed twenty years ago. If you don't actually need to do anything with the wheel itself, my vote is firebomb the place and walk away. Safest for everyone involved."

"I like the way you think." Seth grinned. "How upset do you think Caden will be?"

Nash sighed. "Monster hunting has required Caden to allow for some room to bend the rules. Vernon owns the location, so no one else is getting hurt. The clientele is already technically dead, or the kind of things we kill. It's unlikely to burn down the neighborhood unless we nuke it from space. We've done similar things before." He paused. "Caden might also have some ideas for how we keep random bystanders clear and activate the fire control resources once your team is clear, so the situation doesn't get out of hand."

"Destroying the anchor is one of the most important parts of stopping the disciple," Seth told Nash. "Thank you. Just be careful."

"Some of the ghosts were the monsters' victims," Nash replied.

"They're going to make sure this works and that I'm okay. I promise. Will your part at the turpentine plant go okay without a ghost wrangler?"

"Kinsley is bringing a necromancer, so we should be covered," Seth told him.

"That should work. Be careful, and see you on the flip side."

They thanked him again, and Seth ended the call.

Before either Seth or Evan had time to say anything, they heard the crunch of tires outside the RV.

Evan went to the window to get a look at their visitors. Tony grabbed a large kitchen knife. Seth reached for the gun in the desk drawer as his phone rang, and he answered it. He put the gun back in the drawer and motioned for Tony to put down the knife.

"It's Teag and Rowan," Seth said. He and Evan went to the door to greet their guests.

"Thanks for making a house call," Seth said, although the humor didn't meet his eyes. "And by the way, that's Tony. He's hiding with us for the duration."

Tony waved and went back to cleaning up the kitchen.

"Evan, how do you feel?" Rowan's gaze swept over Evan, making him feel like she could see down to his bones. Teag also studied him with clinical intensity, and Evan wondered how the curse appeared to their magic-enhanced senses.

"All over awful, and like someone pulled my plug," Evan replied. Seth took a step closer, protective as always.

"That fits," Teag said. "I can sense the spell, and it's a nasty piece of work. Dark stuff—worked by someone who has power and knows what he's doing."

"But not invincible." A slight smile touched Rowan's lips. "There are always cracks where the magic isn't quite perfect. I can't break it, but I think I can slow it down and make you more comfortable and functional."

"What do I need to do?" Evan asked.

Rowan smiled reassuringly. "Just stand there and open your mind and soul to my words."

Evan nodded, suddenly feeling out of his depth. "Okay. Ready when you are."

Rowan took a few deep breaths and her expression grew placid. She began to chant in a language Evan didn't recognize, but he could feel the power in her words even if he didn't know their meaning.

He closed his eyes, doing his best to eliminate all resistance and let her magic flow into and through him. At first, it felt like a chill beneath his skin, then heat, and finally a tingle as if he had touched a live wire before the sensation abruptly stopped.

Evan looked at Rowan. "Is that it?"

Seth stood beside him, intrigued and concerned.

She nodded. "Yes. How do you feel?"

Evan searched for words to describe the impact of the spell. "Braced, like I'm not cured, but there's something helping to support me. And the discomfort is less, although I know the problem is still there. Like when you take aspirin, and the headache isn't gone, but it's better."

"Good. That's how it should be. I'm sorry I can't do more." Rowan patted him on the arm like a concerned older sister.

Teag pulled a linen scarf from his pocket, and Evan remembered that Teag's magic could weave spells into cloth. "There are protections against evil and harm worked into the warp and woof," he told Evan as he handed it over. "It should also lessen the effects and buy you time."

Evan wrapped the scarf around his neck and felt his shoulders and back relax, and the tension in his neck eased. A sense of well-being suffused through him, lifting his spirits and driving back the sludgy feeling from dark magic.

"I can feel your magic." Evan turned to Teag, who watched him expectantly. "It's like being wrapped in white light."

"Together, my magic and Rowan's should make the next hours bearable," Teag said. "And when the curse breaks, you'll know right away because all the bad stuff will suddenly stop affecting you. You might be more tired than usual, but you won't feel sick or weakened."

"Thank you so much," Evan said, and Seth echoed his words. "I really appreciate it."

"Any time." Rowan turned to Seth.

"I also brought a spelled knife," Teag added. "It's one we had at Trifles and Folly. Cassidy thought it might help." He handed it to Seth. "You might need this."

"Thank you—for everything," Seth said.

"We're going to go finish up preparations, and we'll see you at dawn," Rowan told them.

Once they drove away, Evan and Seth went back to making calls. After a while, Evan looked up.

"Kinsley's coven is good to go, and so is Tristan the necromancer. They're planning to stay outside the actual site so they can also watch in case Vernon has backup. She promised they've got magic planned that will affect both inside and outside of the building."

"Tristan intends to rally the ghosts. There are a lot of spirits who would love to have a chance to avenge themselves against Vernon. Having Nash and his team—living and ghostly—destroying Vernon's anchor and his monster meat restaurant will make a big difference. Caden has more information about the turpentine factory interior where the ritual is likely to be held," Evan reported. "And he's got some old Army buddies who are willing to provide muscle outside. Said they didn't turn a hair when he asked for their help, despite the early time."

The willingness of their friends to come together despite the danger warmed Evan, although he still felt chagrined at being sidelined. Seth seemed to guess his mood.

"Hey, don't sulk," Seth said as Tony placed plates piled high with cheesy nachos on the table.

"I'm not sulking." Evan realized that he sounded petulant. "I just don't like not being able to have your back."

"I can rig earbuds that give you a live feed, and you can relay information," Seth offered. "And I'll put a drone with a camera in position so you've got a bird's eye view. That gives you intel we won't have on the ground, and it could be important."

"Okay," Evan agreed grudgingly. "I'll do anything I can to help." He took a bite of one of the nachos and moaned, enjoying the taste. "Wow, that's good. Definitely hits the spot."

"Glad to lend a hand." Tony beamed at the compliment.

By unspoken agreement, they worked into the evening, digging into lore that might provide an edge in the coming battle. Evan knew that they should sleep before the fight, but he and Seth both felt the need to search for more to help them tip the balance. For now, he was hanging on, although he still felt unwell. If he couldn't be present at the battle, he resolved not to sleep through the preparations.

He and Seth were surrounded by stacks of old books. Tony sat on the couch, resolutely refusing to rest while they were still up working. He kept them supplied with coffee and made a batch of cookies out of odds and ends from the pantry.

"Here's something," Evan said after a few hours. "This might be helpful. It's a protection spell, but I think it's musical. Hey, Tony, come have a look."

Tony joined them at the table, and Evan passed the book to him. He looked a little confused at first, but then he began to nod.

"I don't know anything about magic, but the melody reminds me of the sort of songs used in rituals and worship. People who believe in that kind of thing say it collects and sends energy." Tony stared at the book with wonder. "I didn't think that was real."

"Very real," Evan assured him. "Can you figure out what the notes are?"

Tony reached for a piece of paper and a pencil from the pile on the table and focused on the yellowed pages of the book. His brows furrowed in concentration, and the tip of his tongue peeked from between his lips.

Evan needed to stretch, so he got up and walked around to see what Seth was working on.

"That's a grimoire," Evan said quietly when he caught sight of the book cover Seth had been studying for the last while.

"Yeah. One of the set we got out of that second-hand shop to pass on to Cassidy," Seth replied. Trifles and Folly made sure problematic tomes didn't land in the wrong hands.

"I thought we agreed it was dark stuff," Evan said, uncomfortable with resorting to questionable magic.

Seth shrugged. "Desperate times, desperate measures. I didn't want to rule out a resource just because some of the contents were iffy. You used the Dark Web to find out more about Vernon's secret restaurant."

"That's not the same as finding spells there. Please don't let the curse and your nightmare push you into using gray magic. That sort of thing always comes around to bite us on the ass." Evan knew how laser-focused Seth could be in a dire situation, and with Evan's life on the line, he feared Seth's concentration might veer into obsession and a willingness to risk too much.

"I'm not going to let you die," Seth replied without looking up. "Or Pax. I'll do whatever it takes to stop this son of a bitch."

"We've never needed to go that far before." Evan pressed a kiss to Seth's temple. "Promise me that you'll discuss anything you find with Milo or Rowan."

"Of course."

It didn't occur to Evan until later that Seth's response wasn't exactly a promise.

Evan went back to skimming another book from his stack, but he kept checking on Tony and Seth since his own search wasn't proving fruitful.

"I think I've got an idea how this works," Tony said after a couple of hours. "It's a bit of a musical riddle, which I guess meant it was coded so it wouldn't be easy for someone without some training to read. But I'm pretty sure I've figured it out."

Evan came to sit next to him on the couch. Seth had taken a break earlier to set up what Evan would need to be in touch during the battle, as well as the camera drone, but otherwise he remained absorbed in his book.

"The old-fashioned wording threw me at first, but I looked up what I needed on my phone." Tony sounded excited about his discovery. "I'll save you the tedious geeky stuff. According to what I could make out, it's a twelve-note sequence and the more you play it with the right instruments, the more power the text says it raises."

Evan nodded. "That makes sense. Three is a powerful number in magic, and so are multiples of three. Twelve is a number for balance and completion—months, signs of the Zodiac, etc."

Tony looked at him. "How do you know this stuff?"

Evan shrugged. "It became my life after Seth saved me and we went on the road. When your survival depends on what you know, you get good at learning new things."

"Makes sense," Tony replied. "I've been into music since before I could read. And I have some goth friends who weren't exactly witches but really liked supernatural stuff. I know that some musical instruments are said to have extra vibes for that sort of thing."

"Oh yeah?" Evan couldn't help being intrigued.

"You know how in every fantasy book the bard has a lute and ends up playing a role against the big bad? I think my guitar is a close substitute," Tony said. "It would help a lot if we could get help from folks who can play the ocarina, flute, and drum."

Evan's excitement dimmed. "We have to be careful about bringing more people into this for their safety as well as ours."

"We can do a video session." Tony's enthusiasm was infectious. "I've got friends in town who would be excited about jamming with us. And if you want to limit the new people, how are you on drums?"

"Passable. I was in a band for a little while back in high school. I can keep a rhythm, but I don't own a drum anymore."

"You can bang on a pot. It will work," Tony assured him. "That's all we need. I can show you the beat. Then we start playing at the right time and repeat to build up the energy. That should help you feel better and also send extra power to Seth for the fight."

"It would be better not to tell your friends what we're really doing if we can avoid it." Evan met Tony's eyes. "I don't want to lie to them, but we don't want to put them in danger."

"We're asking them to play an obscure piece of music at dawn over and over to raise magic. We've got to give them a good reason. They know Pax, and they'll want to help rescue him," Tony countered.

Evan looked from Tony to Seth. "You're right. I guess we're going to have to tell them at least a version of the truth. When should we work the musical spell?"

Seth sat back in his chair, finally pulling his attention away from the grimoire, and drummed his fingers on the table as he thought. "Vernon is an elemental witch, so he can affect the weather. There's supposed to be a storm front coming in tomorrow, and that could feed him extra energy. The music magic could counter that and send us more power."

"How would we know when to start and how long to play?" Tony asked.

"I can signal Evan right before we go in," Seth said. "If you start then and keep playing, maybe we can hijack some of that storm energy, or at least match it."

"My friends love a good jam session," Tony assured them. Despite the late hour, he made several quick calls and found his friends still awake.

Tony explained as much as he could and asked them to be ready at sunrise, which was now only a few hours away. To Evan's surprise, the friends agreed right away, enthusiastic about helping.

Evan yawned and looked at his watch. "We'd better get some sleep. Tomorrow is going to be a rough day."

Seth packed a duffel bag full of everything he would need for spells and combat, including weapons and the grimoire. Evan followed him around, feeling helpless but resolved not to miss a minute of their time together before the battle.

They helped Tony get settled in the living room and set out a towel for him in the bathroom before getting cleaned up and heading for bed. Seth rolled toward Evan, staring at him in the near-darkness.

"How are you feeling? Did Rowan and Teag really help?"

Evan heard the worry in Seth's voice and reached out for him, nestling close with his head against Seth's chest. "Yes, it helped. I can tell that there's something wrong with me, but it's better than it was. And I'll keep pushing through to help as long as I'm able."

"I'm so sorry that Vernon managed to put the whammy on you." Seth's voice was low and intimate in the darkness. "He wasn't trying to make a deal to get us to back off. This is his bid to save himself and the rest of the witch-disciples by stopping us. He figured out that forcing our hand was the only way to do that."

"Please, come back to me." Evan leaned in to kiss Seth, putting all his love, worry, and passion into the press of his lips and the touch of his hands. "I need you."

Seth kissed him, urgent and claiming. "I love you, and I don't want to live without you. I won't let him take you away from me," he promised. "Just hang in there until we stop him. I fail if I don't save you."

"I'll do everything I can to make that happen." Evan sealed his promise with another kiss, then burrowed against Seth, listening to his heartbeat as they finally fell asleep.

THEY WOKE BEFORE DAWN. TONY HAD A FRESH POT OF COFFEE WAITING FOR them, as well as a plate of no-bake oatmeal cookies. He looked haggard but wore a stubborn expression that dared either Seth or Evan to mention it.

"I wanted to have something ready for breakfast." Tony shrugged. "I couldn't sleep."

Seth filled a cup for Evan and then poured one for himself, using the coffee to wash down the cookies. "I wish I could mainline the caffeine." Seth blinked his eyes, struggling to wake up in spite of having doused his face in cold water.

Thunder rumbled in the distance, and Evan heard the patter of rain on the RV's metal roof. "The storm is starting."

Seth took Evan's hand. "Storm energy is neutral—it's not rooting for us or Vernon. He's probably planning to co-opt it, but if you and Tony can make the music magic work, that could make a big difference. It could help us get an edge."

He and Evan had slept fitfully, even though they were always touching in some way throughout the night.

Seth's phone pinged, and he glanced down. "Everyone's ready. I'm meeting up with Rowan and Teag. Kinsley's coven will meet us at the site. We're supposed to swing by to convoy with Caden and their bodyguard folks. Nash has the ghosts lined up, and he's heading for the monster restaurant as soon as the sun is up. I doubt we'll surprise Vernon, but he's going to get hit from all sides. And if he intended to do the ritual tonight, we might get a jump on him, for once."

Seth drained his cup and set it aside. "Time to go."

Evan caught him by the shoulders and kissed him hard, trying to put all his love and hope into the connection. "I love you. Come home safe, and bring Pax with you."

Seth added another peck on the lips. "I have every intention of doing that. Love you too. Watch out for each other. I'll see you when it's over."

With that, Seth picked up the duffel and headed out the door without looking back.

"Get ready," Tony told Evan. "Dawn is in twenty minutes, and the musicians are waiting for a link for the video conference."

EVAN MADE A QUICK PASS THROUGH THE BATHROOM TO WASH HIS FACE with cold water and get dressed. As the sun rose, Evan's phone pinged with a call from Seth. He put in an earbud and checked his signal strength.

"We're in position," Seth told him. "You should be able to pick up on the drone feed in a couple of minutes."

"The musicians are ready to play the spell," Evan told him. "Let me connect to the drone, and I can tell you what I see."

Evan pulled up the drone's video feed. He guessed that Seth had flown it in through a hole in the building's ceiling because he could see rafters where it had perched. That meant Vernon's people might not notice the robot, but it had as good a view of the battle zone as possible.

As Evan adjusted the angle of the camera, he saw an empty industrial space that looked like it once held vats and piping. A ritual area had been set up with sigils painted on the floor and pillar candles set at intervals around the workspace.

Pax hung suspended by chains, dangling in the middle of the large warded circle. He wasn't moving, but the lack of blood assured Evan that the ritual hadn't begun yet.

"Pax, oh my God," Tony gasped.

"I've got a visual." Evan filled Seth in on what he saw. "Someone had to light the candles, so I'm guessing at least a few of Vernon's coven members are present but out of sight. I can't tell if Pax is breathing, but he's not bleeding heavily." He paused. "There's something inside the warding, along with two guards—large men—be careful. Whatever the other thing is, it doesn't look human. More of a dark shape, but it moves wrong to be a person."

"Noted. Thanks. And remember, they need Pax alive for the ritual," Seth's voice sounded soft and staticky through the earpiece. "We're not too late."

"We should have the music spell going in about five minutes," Evan said.

"We'll be on the move by then. Keep the chatter on this line minimal, but if you see something, let me know. You've got the bird's eye view."

"Good luck." Evan instilled the two words with everything he felt. *I love you. I need you. Please be safe.*

"You, too." Seth's tone told Evan everything he needed to know.

Evan glanced at Tony, who looked pale and shaken. "Are you okay?"

"Hell, no. Pax..." He swallowed hard. "I want to kill those motherfuckers and make sure Pax comes home safely."

Tony pulled up his laptop and opened the video conference program, sending the link to Evan and the others. Evan had already tried it to make sure he could keep the drone feed separate from the group program. He would be able to monitor the scene, but the others would not share his screen.

"Here." Tony handed Evan the empty spaghetti pot from under the stove. "You're officially our drummer."

One by one, Tony's friends popped up on the screen. "Ava, Josh, Tim, this is Evan. Evan, meet the gang." Everyone smiled and waved, exchanging greetings.

Despite the early hour, everyone looked remarkably awake, or maybe they hadn't yet been to bed. Ava had dark eyes and brown hair in a ponytail. Evan guessed she was the flute player. Josh pushed a comb into his bushy black hair and gave them a broad grin as he held up his ocarina.

"Ready when you are, boss," Josh said.

Tim was a pale ginger with curly hair and light blue eyes, and Evan could easily imagine him and his lute cosplaying at a Renaissance festival. "I went over the score you sent. It's odd. How about telling us what's really going on? You don't usually want to jam before sunrise."

Evan and Tony exchanged a look. Tony gave an encouraging nod, and Evan threw caution to the wind.

"Go for it," Evan said, shrugging.

Tony cleared his throat. "I told you about Pax getting kidnapped by a witch who wants to hurt him. The witch also cursed Evan. Evan's partner and their friends went to rescue Pax and stop the witch, but they need all the help they can get. I know there's no reason for you to believe me, but this song is a type of spell that can send energy to the good guys to help them power up."

Tony's friends blinked at them in silence for a minute, and Evan braced himself for them to break out laughing or call Tony out on playing a joke.

"I told you it was some sort of magic," Tim said to the others.

"This is so cool," Ava chimed in. "I've seen this kind of thing on TV, but I didn't think it actually worked."

"We're here for you," Josh added. "Let's play."

Tony grinned. "You guys are the best. Thank you."

Evan put one of Seth's shirts on his lap beneath the drum to direct the spell's energy to the right recipient. The source also mentioned cleansing, and Evan hoped that the magic might ease the curse since he was part of the casting.

"We need to pace ourselves," Tony told them. "We want to play for at least an hour—as long as we possibly can. Start easy and feel the music. If we go faster later on, that's okay. We just have to keep it up."

"On three," Tim said, and they readied their instruments. "One. Two. Three."

The simple melody took on richer notes as all the instruments joined in. Tony had coached Evan on the rhythm he thought would work best, and Evan poured his will and concentration into maintaining the beat and adding to the harmony.

The first several repetitions didn't feel like anything special. Evan began to worry that they had gotten it all wrong. But on the twelfth cycle, Evan felt energy begin to rise.

"Do you feel that?" Tony asked. "Keep going, it's starting to build."

Outside, the rain had picked up, adding a droning undertone to the song.

"We're playing," Evan said quietly to Seth, not sure how much Seth could hear of the music. "Sending the music magic your way. Hope it helps."

"Keep it up," Seth murmured into the link. "The power is building."

Evan kept up the beat as muscle memory kicked in, helping him stay with the others. On the screen, he saw figures he guessed to be Seth, Rowan, Teag, and Caden walk into view. Kinsley's coven would remain outside, while Caden's friends locked down the area. If all went well, Nash and the ghosts would join them after they destroyed the anchor.

Seth and the others stayed in the shadows near the door, awaiting Vernon's entrance. So far, the two guards inside the warded area hadn't seemed to notice that Seth's team had entered. That made Evan guess Seth's people had used borrowed magic to cloak their approach.

"He's coming," Evan murmured when he spotted Vernon and his coven enter from the far side of the opening.

Vernon and the others didn't bother with robes and hoods, dressed instead in black shirts and pants; each of them wearing identical large amulets. Evan couldn't make out the shape of the necklaces, but he guessed them to be wrought of silver and bone.

"We welcome our honored guest," Vernon said as he stepped into the warded circle and approached where Pax hung, motionless.

"I know you're awake. Pretend all you like; you'll give us what we came for before we're through."

Vernon paused, then he raised his face and slowly turned in place until he locked his gaze on the drone.

"Is that you, Evan Malone? There's not much time left for you. Goodbye."

With that, the drone's camera flared white and then went dark.

"Drone's down," Evan said. "Audio from your team only."

"Just play the music. We'll handle the rest." Seth's mic clicked off.

Evan felt a moment of panic before realizing that hearing the battle without any reference to what was happening would be torturous. Still, he hated not knowing what was going on or that Seth was still alive.

Tony met his gaze. "Put everything you've got into the song. That's how we can save them."

Evan had kept up the beat despite everything, and now he closed his eyes and focused on the drumming, breathing deeply to still his thoughts.

Nothing matters except the song. The beat. Keep playing. Send the energy. Save them.

The song cycled again and again, and Evan felt the magic rise and build. He suspected it would feel even stronger if all the musicians were together in the same place, and hoped that doing it this way would be enough.

Outside, the wind howled, and rain lashed the RV, loud on the aluminum walls. Evan wondered if he was imagining that the storm and the song seemed to build at the same time.

He lost track of time, swept up in the beat, the song, and the rain. The forecast had called for showers but not a torrential downpour, nor had it mentioned the lightning that flared in the sky or the thunder that shook the RV.

Evan kept an image of Seth and Pax in his mind as he drummed, doing his best to will the rising magic toward them.

Seth said Vernon was an elemental mage. If the song co-opts energy from the storm, does it weaken the power Vernon has available to draw on? Maybe we're not just strengthening the magic for Seth's witches, we're also draining a resource Vernon might have counted on using. And if we're right about the ship's wheel being Vernon's anchor, destroying that will also give us an edge, and sap Vernon's magic even more.

Outside, the sky lightened from black to muddy gray as dawn came. Strong winds whipped around the RV, rocking it from side to side and making Evan fear that despite physical tethers and protective magic, they might be knocked over. The rain beat against the windows, making it impossible to see.

Save Seth. Save Pax. Lift the curse. Save Seth. Save Pax, Lift the curse.

The words became a mantra he silently chanted in time with the music. Tony played with a look of resolute concentration, and Evan guessed that the musician was similarly fixed on channeling himself into the rescue.

Despite being drawn into their last-minute effort, Tony's friends played with enthusiasm. From their expressions of peaceful concentration, they looked like they were equally swept into the surge of the magic as the power rose.

We can't win the battle for Seth, but maybe we'll be the extra edge that makes the difference.

Unbidden, Evan's mind supplied its own images of the battle, filling in from imagination what the drone no longer showed.

Vernon and his coven would use every bit of dark power they possessed to hold off Seth's attack and work the ritual. Evan only remembered bits and pieces from his own rescue, but the attacks he and Seth had mounted to save the other descendants remained clear in his mind.

He remembered the smell of the herbs and potions and the scent of the candle smoke. Evan had been bound to a table while Pax hung from chains, but Evan could still feel the bite of cold iron on his wrists. Despite being drugged, he had been utterly terrified. He hoped that Pax was indeed unconscious and spared that terror and the dreams that followed.

Evan's hands ached from the constant drumming, but he kept on playing, welcoming the pain that reminded him he was still alive. The magic had eased some of the discomfort from the curse, but Evan knew it still drained him.

The song took on a life of its own, skirling high and dropping low, in tune with their breath and heartbeats. Evan had read about monks who played for spiritual transcendence, but until now he had never understood how such a thing could be possible.

Now, he believed.

If we didn't have people to rescue, would the song put good energy out into the world to heal what's broken?

If he survived, Evan promised himself he would ask Rowan about the possibility.

The storm raged on, and thunder rattled the windows in the RV.

Tony flinched at the sound but never lost the melody. Evan realized they had been playing for over an hour and wondered how much longer the fight would last.

Evan felt himself fading and clung to the music magic to keep him from collapsing. He worried that meant the battle wasn't going well, and fear tightened his chest and nearly took his breath away.

Winning was never assured, no matter how good their magic or how powerful their allies. Yet Evan had never let himself imagine not freeing Pax and stopping Vernon and his followers. Now, he worried that their effort might not be enough.

Seth has weapons and charms. Teag and Rowan are powerful witches, and so are Kinsley and her coven. He's got Caden and some muscle for backup, plus Tristan and Nash to summon the ghosts to help.

It's got to be enough. Please, let it be enough.

The sun was fully up now, lifting the gloom despite the rain that continued unabated. The wind had died down, and the thunder and lightning stopped. Evan didn't know whether that was an omen tied to the magic or just a storm running its course.

Tony glanced toward him and frowned. "Doing okay?"

Evan guessed his dwindling reserves showed in his face. "Yeah. Hanging in there."

Although he continued to play, Evan felt as if the music was all that sustained him. He knew he couldn't keep going much longer.

Did we fail? Did Seth stop Vernon before he killed Pax?

Evan searched his feelings, but was unsure how to separate his own imagination from anything he might be reading from the magic.

The song slowed from its frantic peak as the rain slacked off. Evan didn't know if the magic affected the storm, but they certainly seemed intertwined at the climax of the magic.

Reluctantly, Evan sensed that the song's power was spent. "I think that's it, folks," he told the others. One by one they stopped playing.

"Did it work?" Ava asked, and the others looked on with concern.

"No way to know until we hear back," Tony told them. "I know that we helped. I have to believe it made a difference. Thank you all so much."

"Let us know how Pax is," Tim said. Now that they were no longer playing, everyone looked tired from the early hour and the energy poured into the magic.

"I will. Go rest," Tony told them. "And light a candle, or however you send good vibes. We need all the luck we can get."

His friends closed their video windows, and Tony shut down his laptop. He looked at Evan with concern.

"I take it the tech didn't work?"

Evan shook his head. "Vernon spotted the drone and shut it down. Seth turned off the audio feed since I didn't have intel for them, and without the video feed, it would just be noise. But I hate not knowing."

"I have to believe that they'll win." Tony looked as scared as Evan felt. "I refuse to think anything else until we know for certain."

"I've always been with Seth during the fight—even the first time, when I was the sacrifice," Evan replied. "While I might have been in mortal danger, at least I knew what was going on."

He sighed. "They haven't beaten Vernon yet. I'd feel it."

"Give them time," Tony urged.

Tony put his guitar to one side and moved their laptops. "Why don't you lie down? I'll sit in the chair, and that way we'll be on hand when they get back."

"But you're sleeping here," Evan protested. Tony had stripped the pull-out bed and refolded it into a couch before they started to play.

Tony gave him a look. "There's no way I'm going to get back to sleep after all that, and you probably don't want to be back in the bedroom until they come home." He frowned. "We both should eat something. The spell took a lot of energy from both of us, and you were already dealing with the curse. Sit tight, and I'll rustle up some food."

"Thank you." Evan accepted that Tony was right, both about resting and eating, although he didn't want to do either. But fidgeting or pacing wouldn't change anything, and he didn't want to drain himself even more in case killing Vernon didn't end the curse.

Evan didn't lie down, but he got comfortable propped up on pillows. To his surprise, he drifted off into a fitful sleep. His mind conjured images from what little the drone had shown him, envisioning how the fight might have gone. In some versions, Seth and his allies won, rescuing Pax. In others, Vernon prevailed.

Evan woke with a start from one of the darker scenarios to find Tony sitting on the edge of the couch, gently shaking his shoulder.

"Sorry to wake you, but it didn't seem like you were having a good time," Tony said with a lightheartedness that didn't reach his eyes.

"I made more coffee, and I figure you can't go wrong with toast and jam." He indicated a cup and plate on the end table. "Go ahead and eat. I don't want to explain to Seth that I let you pass out."

Evan sat up and stirred extra sugar into his coffee and drank it like an elixir, letting it warm him from the inside and drive away the chill that came with the aftermath of magic. He didn't realize how much the spell had taken out of him and wondered to what degree the curse made it worse.

"How do you feel?" he asked Tony before he nibbled at the toast. "You should eat too."

"I already ate," Tony replied. "You were out cold. I feel tired, like I did a hard workout, but also jittery, like I had too many energy drinks. It's an odd combination, but I'm guessing it's from what it took to work the magic."

Evan nodded. "Magic concentrates and redirects energy, but it doesn't create it out of nothing. That's part of the danger for the witch. Without enough preparation or if they don't pay close attention, they can drain themselves to death. It's why destroying his anchor and amulet is so important."

Tony smiled. "I know the circumstances are awful, but I'm still blown away by having actually worked a spell. I thought that was just in books."

Evan took a few more bites and gulped some coffee before he replied. "That's how I felt when I first got involved with Seth. Now, we have so many friends who do all kinds of supernatural things that I guess I've gotten used to it."

"Should we have heard from them by now?" Tony asked.

Evan could see the fear in Tony's eyes for Pax and knew the musician was unnerved by all the unfamiliar things that were going on around him. He appreciated Tony's kindness in looking out for him despite his own apprehension.

"We'll hear when we hear," Evan replied. Despite his comforting words and positive attitude toward Tony, Evan worried about the same things.

"There's no telling what could be happening around them that might not even involve Vernon, like dodging the police. We have to hang tight." Evan hoped with everything in him that their friends would win the battle.

5

SETH

Seth hated walking away from Evan and leaving him behind, although he knew that Evan wasn't up to joining the fight this time. If Evan went with them to confront Vernon and the curse took its toll, it could be a fatal distraction for them all.

His dream the night before about Jesse made the guilt over not being able to save him sting fresh and sharp. That just made Seth even more determined not to fail Evan.

He said a silent prayer that Evan and Tony could take care of each other. And he said another to any god who might be listening that the dubious spell he had memorized from the grimoire would work.

Evan was right, gray magic was dangerous. That term applied to spells that didn't require horrific elements like human or animal sacrifice but which drew on other questionable sources to increase their power. That might mean tapping the life energy of unwilling donors short of draining them dry. It might also involve summoning storms for a boost, which could break free of the witch's control and cause death or damage.

Most ethical witches also considered spells that were overtly suicidal to be undesirable for obvious reasons.

All magic drew on the casting witch's life energy to some extent.

Part of learning magic lay in knowing personal limitations and not pushing too far. Ethical witches found other sources of additional power—natural energy wells, ways to store magic for future use, and working with a willing partner—to extend their ability.

Like the music magic Tony and Evan were using to sustain Teag and Rowan.

The spell Seth had found drew on the caster's and target's life force, which would allow him to siphon away the witch-disciple's power. It took the target's magic and allowed the caster to imbue it into a blade, making the weapon more lethal.

If the spell gave them enough of an advantage, maybe they could kill Vernon before the gray magic drained Seth dry, and Evan would be free.

If not, Seth wouldn't be left behind, and maybe his soul and Evan's would find each other in the afterlife.

He knew Evan disapproved. Seth respected Evan's feelings, but letting him die without a fight wasn't going to happen. He felt guilty that he didn't ask Milo or Rowan about the spell as Evan requested, nor had he been fully upfront with Teag and Rowan about the source.

Seth felt certain that Teag and Rowan wouldn't be happy, but they would understand. He didn't care about the price as long as Evan lived.

"Heading your way," Seth said on the phone to Caden as he drove toward the turpentine plant.

"You think that new tech stuff will work?" Caden asked. Seth had gone over the drone and earbuds with him beforehand, planning to use off-the-shelf gear.

"Maybe," Seth admitted. "If it does, that's an advantage we didn't have before. We've also got some music magic adding to the energy." What he couldn't say because Evan was listening was that he wanted Evan and Tony to feel like they were part of the effort so they didn't insist on coming along.

"I'm all for progress," Caden said. "And Nash is driving separately. He said he needed the ghosts for a diversion."

"Is everyone in place?" Seth asked.

"Teag and Rowan are here with me, and so are my friends," Caden replied. "Kinsley's got her people set up, Tristan is checking out the area, and Nash and the ghosts will join us when he finishes his side quest. We should be good to go when you get here."

"Roger that." Seth ended the call so he could focus on driving, keeping watch for anything that might suggest Vernon had called in extra help.

Nothing looked out of the ordinary, but Seth knew he couldn't let his guard down. Vernon had thrown down the gauntlet, so he knew they were coming. Either he didn't believe they could harm him—incredible hubris considering the track record Seth and Evan had with the other witch-disciples—or he felt confident enough in his own plans to draw them in before he made his move.

Just before dawn, Seth joined the others in an alley a block away from the turpentine plant. "Thanks, everyone. It's going to take all of us to shut down Vernon for good."

Kinsley's coven had taken up monitoring points all around the plant, and Tristan had moved into position. Seth and his strike force were waved inside the perimeter by a large man standing sentry, one of Caden's military buddies. Caden, Teag, and Rowan reflected the same mix of apprehension and battle energy that Seth felt.

"Remember," Seth told them, momentarily toggling off his link to Evan. "Vernon put a killing curse on Evan. Either we kill Vernon, or Evan dies. I'll do whatever it takes to stop Vernon. If it comes down to me or Evan, well, I'm going to save Evan. And I've got a plan."

He turned to Teag. "Nash and his ghosts went after Vernon's anchor. Destroying that will weaken him. Tristan will marshal the ghosts here. And remember that grimoire I told you about? The one I'm planning to bring to the store?"

Teag's expression turned wary. "We have no idea about the origin—"

"I found something that I think I can do that will help," Seth said. "Desperate times and all that."

"There's always a cost," Rowan warned.

"Can't be worse than losing Evan," Seth countered. "I'm willing to take that chance because I can't live with the alternative."

Seth activated the comm link as he pulled the drone from a tote bag and turned it on. "We're in position," Seth said to Evan. "You should be able to pick up on the drone feed in a couple of minutes."

"The musicians are ready to play the spell," Evan responded. "Let me connect to the drone, and I can tell you what I see."

The drone flew into the plant and then headed to the rafters, settling where it had a bird's eye view of the main floor.

"I've got a visual," Evan said over the link. "Someone had to light the candles, so I'm guessing at least a few of Vernon's coven are present but out of sight. I can't tell if Pax is breathing, but he's not bleeding heavily." He paused. "There's something inside the warding, along with two guards—large men—be careful. Whatever the other thing is, it doesn't look human. More of a dark shape, but it moves wrong to be a person."

"Noted. Thanks. And remember, they need Pax alive for the ritual. We're not too late," Seth assured.

"We should have the music spell going in about five minutes," Evan said.

"We'll be on the move by then. Keep the chatter on this line minimal, but if you see something, let me know. You've got the bird's eye view."

"Good luck."

"You, too."

Seth glanced over to Teag, Rowan, and Caden. "It's go time."

Outside, thunder rumbled, and rain began to ping against the building's steel roof. Teag and Seth led the way, with Rowan and Caden behind them.

"He's this way," Teag murmured. "I can feel the magic."

Rusted machinery and heavy cobwebs made it clear that the old factory hadn't been used in a long time. Even so, the smell of turpentine permeated the building, sunk into the wooden floors.

"There wasn't a storm expected today," Rowan said quietly. "Someone's conjured what's out there. And it's getting stronger."

"Evan said there's a ritual space where the main factory area used to be," Seth reported via the headset. "Pax is hanging from chains in the middle of a warded circle. No sign yet of Vernon and the others."

"It sounds like everything is ready for the ceremony—lit candles, bowls of materials," Teag added. "Watch yourselves. Vernon's got to be heading there any minute."

"We're playing," Evan said over the link. "Sending the music magic your way. Hope it helps." In the background, Seth heard the sound of drums, a guitar, and a flute.

Rowan caught Seth's eye and nodded. "Faint so far, but I can feel it," she replied, following the conversation on her earbud.

"Keep it up," Seth murmured to Evan. "The power is building."

"Let's go," Seth said to the others. "This might be our best chance to get to Pax."

"Think it's a trap?" Caden asked.

"No way to know." The thought had crossed Seth's mind. Despite their research, Vernon was still largely a mystery. Whether the witch would alter his schedule out of fear that Seth and the others could disrupt him depended on his hubris, although Seth figured Vernon had to know that he and Evan had shut down a growing number of the disciples.

But there's always the one who figures it won't happen to him. Vernon's that kind of guy.

Outside, the storm grew louder, and Seth wondered how much was due to Vernon's magic. Kinsley's witches targeted Vernon to siphon away his mojo. If they could break Vernon's hold on the storm, it could replenish Seth, Teag, and Rowan since the energy itself was neutral. Meanwhile, Tristan's necromancy gathered the angry ghosts eager for revenge.

"There's something not human inside the warding," Seth cautioned. "Got any idea what it is before we have to fight it?"

"The ghosts say there's a wraith guarding Pax as well as some of his witches," Tristan warned over the link. "Don't let it get you."

Seth glanced to Teag and Rowan, who nodded to let him know that they heard the message. Wraiths were nasty pieces of work, and Seth wasn't thrilled to add one to the mix of adversaries they already had to overcome.

"Let's go." Seth and Caden carried regular handguns as well as knives and a few other surprises. Teag and Rowan also had daggers, but their real defense lay in their magic.

"The wraith is in the shadows," Rowan murmured, and the headset let her voice carry to them all despite the quiet volume. "The circle is warded, so don't try to cross it until Teag and I can dismantle that. I'll go after the wraith."

"And I'll hit Vernon and the witches," Teag added. "The rest of you —work the plan."

They sounded confident that their magic was up to the challenge, boosting Seth's hopes. But even with his powerful friends and their helpers outside, Seth knew better than to take a win for granted.

The energy suddenly shifted, like a fresh wind sweeping away a dark, fetid cloud. Seth could feel the fundamental change.

"Anchors aweigh," Nash said over the headset, confirming Seth's guess.

Nash did it. We were right. The ship's wheel was the anchor, and he's destroyed it.

"They've knocked out the anchor, and I can feel the music magic," Teag said. "It's building, and within reach when we need it."

That helped since Vernon had his coven, who at the very least, served as an energy source for the witch-disciple. Seth doubted Vernon trusted witches of serious power to be in his inner circle, but even those with limited abilities and the right spell could be a danger.

"He's coming," Evan warned, and Seth's group stopped in their tracks.

"We welcome our honored guest." Vernon stepped into the warded circle and approached where Pax hung, motionless.

"I know you're awake," he said to Pax, who did not respond. "Pretend all you like; you'll give us what we came for before we're through."

Vernon slowly turned in place until he locked his gaze on the drone. "Is that you, Evan Malone? There's not much time left for you. Goodbye."

Seconds later, Evan spoke through Seth's headset. "Drone's down. Audio from your team only."

"Just play. We'll handle the rest." Seth told him and ended the connection to Evan.

"Vernon saw the drone and took it out. We're blind. Sorry," Seth told the others.

While the loss of the drone was inconvenient, he wasn't surprised that Vernon had sensed the drone's presence. Seth had switched off Evan's audio feed since it would be awful for him to hear the battle without actually knowing what was going on.

They moved in fast and hard. Rowan lashed a streak of fire against the wraith, which lunged toward them from the shadows, slipping through the warded circle that kept Seth and his friends from reaching Vernon. Vernon and six witches were safe within the circle that held Pax, and from the witch-disciple's expression, he seemed to be relishing the confrontation.

"Watch out!" Seth shouted as the wraith dodged the flames and headed toward Teag.

Teag pivoted and hurled a handful of iron filings from his pocket at the creature, which screamed as the metal touched it, shrinking in on itself just enough for Rowan to attack again.

The wraith shrieked as Rowan's hand-lightning struck it, sending it up in flames.

One down, Seth thought.

Rowan and Teag brought the warded circle down. Before the others could react, Teag brandished a complex piece of spelled weaving, adding a flash of magicked light to make them look at him. Once they did, the web of the woven piece wouldn't let them look away and knocked them out. Teag bound and gagged them, hoping that Vernon could not draw on their power with them unconscious.

Seth shot one of the guards in the chest, and Rowan's lightning struck the second guard, dropping him to the floor. Vernon snarled, and he motioned for the witches to attack.

Ghosts surged from everywhere at once. Some went after the two witches inside the circle with Vernon, while others attacked the remaining six coven members who had not been hit in the first round and were hiding among the equipment.

The coven members might not be as strong as Vernon, but they possessed enough magic to defend themselves and to present a threat to both the ghosts and the rescuers.

One of the coven members sent a streak of fire at Caden, who leaped out of the way, rolled, and came back up firing his gun. His bullet caught the witch in the chest, sending him backward with a growing bloodstain on his shirt.

Seth dodged a ball of blue energy lobbed by another of the witches and shot back, hitting the man in the shoulder. Unlike the wraith, the witches were flesh and blood adversaries, and mortal, as they sometimes forgot.

With two of their number bloodied, four downed by Teag's spell, and Vernon clearly focused on Pax's sacrifice instead of their defense, the remaining witches abandoned their dead and wounded comrades to hide behind machinery.

Seth didn't have the level of innate magical talent that Rowan and Teag did, but the spells he learned by rote still served him well. Knowing that the showdown with Vernon loomed in the future, Seth chose to rely on his gun and save his spells for later.

"Seth, behind you!" Caden warned as he took a shot at another of the witches. He missed, but the man retreated out of sight behind a large distilling kettle.

Seth wheeled, aimed, and shot at a coven member hunched behind a piece of machinery.

Rattling overhead drew Seth's attention just in time to see a piece of ductwork shear loose from its fastening and plummet toward where Caden stood.

"Move!" he shouted to Caden, giving him a shove toward safety while Rowan blasted the falling hunk of metal and sent it out of the way.

"Duck!" Caden yelled, and Seth dropped. Caden fired past him, and while the shot went wide, it forced the attacking witch from cover. Seth didn't miss with his own bullet, and the witch staggered back, bleeding.

Seth heard chanting and hoped that the amulets and protections he and Caden wore would deflect whatever the coven threw at them. A wave of nausea rolled over him but slid away without doing damage, and seconds later, a gurgle deep in his belly faded without harm, thanks to the talismans.

Despite the magic he had used, Seth wasn't as tired as he expected, and he credited the music magic Evan and Tony conjured, as well as whatever power Kinsley and her coven were sending their way. That just reinforced what Seth had learned in battle conditions both magical and mundane—the combined power of a good team was damn near unstoppable. He hoped that applied not only to their witch friends but to the ghosts he would need to make the grimoire spell work.

"Kinsley?" he said into his headset, on high alert for whatever the coven might attempt next.

"There's a bunch of Vernon's mob guys out here. Sorry, taking a lot to hold them off. Some have magic. They sent an exhaustion spell toward us. We blocked it, but it took a toll. Tristan is siccing most of the ghosts on Vernon and some of them against the toughs. We're sending you all we can and still hold off the goons. Good luck," she said before her feed went silent.

That meant reinforcements inside the plant weren't coming soon.

Fire streaked toward Seth, and he barely threw himself to the ground in time to avoid it. Caden shot toward the fire's origin.

"Got him!" Caden shouted.

"Stop the rest of his coven. We'll handle Vernon." Teag's voice came across the earpiece. With Evan's life on the line as well as Pax's, Seth hated not going after the witch-disciple directly, but he knew Teag and Rowan had a much better chance.

Four of the witches were still at large, and while Kinsley's draining spell might be sapping their power, they still remained a danger.

"You'll have to do better than that," Vernon taunted. Although he had Pax in position for the ritual, Vernon hadn't started the magic yet, distracted by their attack. Vernon had conjured a smaller warding over himself and Pax, a faintly glowing translucent dome. Teag loosened one of the stored energy knots on his belt and sent a wave of magic toward the warding, which lit up as it intercepted the threat. Rowan followed up a moment later with a strike in a different color of light, a concerted effort to wear down Vernon's protections.

Outside, the rain pounded on the factory's roof, and the wind howled, echoing in the large, mostly empty building.

Seth called on one of the memorized spells Rowan taught him, a "parasite" incantation that leeched power from another mage's casting. A blue spot appeared on Vernon's dome like mold on cheese, draining magical energy.

Before Vernon had a chance to react, Seth sent a second small spell, this time to cause heat. A red spot appeared next to the blue one, using its power to increase the temperature inside.

Seth knew that something as small as a burr could make a horse buck its rider, and gambled that minor destructive spells, taken together, could help breach Vernon's protections.

At least it will force him to deal with the annoyance, and that means he can't start the ritual.

He took comfort in knowing that whatever else Vernon might do to use the weather against their allies outside, he didn't dare use lightning in a factory full of old boxes and flammable residue.

Before the audio connection ended, Seth had heard the musical spell Evan and Tony wove. Now, he imagined that he felt an outside force buoy his energy, giving him strength to conjure more magic to keep Vernon distracted.

The red spot and the blue spot disappeared from the dome, but Seth sent a freeze cantrip that would make the temperature inside Vernon's protected area plummet from the sweltering heights of the heat spell. He silently apologized to Pax for the discomfort, but figured if the other man lived through the ordeal, he was likely to forgive Seth the inconvenience.

Rowan cast salvo after salvo against the warding to weaken its walls. Seth suspected that Teag drew on extra energy stored in the braided and knotted cords that hung from his belt, part of his Weaver magic.

Seth was so fixed on attacking the dome that he didn't see one of Vernon's coven break from his hiding place until a blast of magic hit and sent him reeling.

He hurled a throwing knife, pegging the witch in the throat. Blood gushed, soaking the man's shirt, and the witch fell back.

Seth felt certain that without his protective amulets, the magical attack would have stopped his heart. He took cover, trying to catch his breath, drawing from the tide of energy supplied by the music Evan and Tony played.

Teag spared a glance to assure that Seth wasn't dead, but didn't pause his incantation. Rowan's cold blasts of magic struck the dome again and again.

Seth forced himself to his feet and spotted one of Vernon's witches circling behind Rowan. The witch saw him first and called out a word of power, opening a gash on Seth's left arm as if he had struck with a blade.

Seth fired his gun, and the shot echoed like thunder in the old building. Magic didn't save the coven member from a spelled bullet intended to incapacitate, but not kill. Seth paused long enough to tie his sleeve around the gash to stanch the bleeding before he returned to the hunt. They would collect the wounded and magic-neutralized witch later, to stand trial among his peers.

Kinsley's draining spell against Vernon's witches may have taken away their most powerful magic, but what remained could be just as deadly.

Seth glimpsed Tristan slipping inside the old plant. His light-blond hair was wild and windblown. Seth moved silently and saw another witch bloodied but still fighting. Just as he leveled his gun, a tide of ghosts surged forward, surrounding the witch who screamed as they clawed him to pieces. Teag flinched, but never stopped repeating his litany.

Thanks, Tristan. Eleven down—one to go.

Seth hoarded his memorized spells for when they would make the most impact because he could only use them once each. He knew better than to try to shoot through the dome. The bullet was likely to ricochet, introducing a new danger.

Vernon's feeding the storm to keep the protectors outside occupied. He's maintaining the dome and the curse on Evan. He's lost all but one of his coven. Nash's ghosts knocked out the anchor, and Tristan is sending a mob of ghosts against him, so even if Vernon beats us, he can't draw on its power to protect himself and work the spell. He's got to know that we've won, but he won't surrender.

Another scream rang out as a storm of angry ghosts got their vengeance. "That's the last of the witches," Caden said through the earpiece.

"Give it up," Seth shouted to Vernon as Rowan and Teag focused their magic on breaking the warding. "It's over."

Vernon's protective dome flickered, no longer as bright as before. Their attacks had taken a toll, badly weakening the witch-disciple, who still remained defiant.

"Aren't you forgetting something?" Vernon taunted. "If you want to save Evan, you've got to kill me."

Vernon looked haggard. Pax remained unconscious, but with the rest of his coven dead and Vernon unable to tap into their power, the ritual couldn't happen. They'd saved Pax, but Vernon surely still had enough mojo to pose a serious threat one-on-one, and clearly intended to do as much damage as possible despite his impending defeat.

Teag and Rowan had stopped their attacks, but their worried expressions let Seth know what they thought about him going up against Vernon.

"I have to." Seth hoped they could understand and resolved to see this through. "I've got to save Evan." *Avenge me if I fail.*

"Let us bring Pax out, safe and alive," Seth called to Vernon. "Let my friends go. I'll fight you. Just the two of us."

"Seth, you can't," Rowan protested.

"You're also a descendant," Teag reminded him. "He could use you like he intended to use Pax."

"I don't think he's got the juice for it," Seth replied. "And I've got a trick or two up my sleeve."

Teag and Rowan clearly didn't like the situation, but Teag gave a tight-lipped nod.

Seth met their gaze. "Get Pax and the others out of here. I'll see you on the other side."

"Lose your nerve, old man?" Seth taunted Vernon. "Send out Pax and let's get this party started."

Vernon released the manacles that held Pax suspended. He dropped to the floor, unconscious. The witch hauled Pax's body to the edge of the dome and rolled him outside like refuse. Teag edged close enough to pull Pax clear while Rowan covered them with magical protections and helped to drag the would-be sacrifice away.

Seth feared that he wouldn't survive his confrontation with Vernon, and rued the consequence even though it had always been a possibility.

Outside, the storm raged, feeding its power to Vernon and rattling the loose sheet steel of the abandoned plant's roof.

How many times have I told Evan that I didn't want to live without him? Vernon has to die for Evan to survive. That's probably going to kill me. But for me, there's no choice at all between saving Evan and losing him. I'm only sorry to leave him on his own.

Seth gripped the spelled knife Teag had given him, one that made his small flicker of magic more powerful. He gave a plea to Tristan over the headset for backup from the ghosts of Vernon's victims, the spirits that surrounded them throughout the fight.

"I need your help to beat him, but if you help me, we can finally destroy Vernon and keep him from hurting anyone ever again," Seth told Tristan. "Lend me your energy. Make me your weapon. I'll be your vengeance."

"Please don't let him win."

Everything seemed to happen at once. Ghosts swept through Seth, chilling him to the bone, gathering strength from Tristan's necromancy and Seth's life energy. They swarmed toward Vernon like a roiling gray cloud.

If the ghosts destroyed Vernon before Seth was completely drained dry, Seth won—and both saved Evan and survived the fight. If not, Seth wouldn't be around to feel his loss.

Vernon wanted a fight to the death. Seth brought him one, although from how Vernon recoiled, clearly the dark witch had felt it was a sucker's bet.

Vernon just never expected to be the sucker.

Seth saw the glint of silver at Vernon's throat. He seized the moment while Vernon was caught off guard by the ghosts' attack. Seth lunged to grab the amulet's chain and yank it hard enough to cut flesh, snapping the chain and sending the protective talisman flying out of Vernon's reach and into the shadows of the old plant.

It's time. Seth silently repeated the memorized spell from the grimoire. He felt a wave of nausea as the magic responded, and he focused on the blade Teag had given him. It began to glow. The dark magic Seth worked helped further drain Vernon's power and his life energy, opening a rip in the protective bubble. He hoped it was enough to give him the chance to kill Vernon with the bespelled knife. The vampiric spell drew from Seth's life energy as well as Vernon's, and carried the taint of blood magic, downsides Seth was willing to accept if he could save Evan and Pax.

Thanks to Tristan's necromancy, Seth let him take over marshaling the spirits of Vernon's prior sacrifices, who filled the abandoned factory, angry and ready for vengeance.

Flurries of consciousness brushed Seth's mind in the onslaught of ghosts. With Vernon weakened and caught off guard by the destruction of his anchor and the loss of his amulet, the spirits of his victims from his century-long existence seized their chance for vengeance as Tristan strengthened their manifestation.

Apparently, Vernon had never considered them a danger since he took no measures to dispel them. Now, they formed an angry storm cloud eager for recompense.

Too many to count.

Seth knew these had to be only a fraction of the souls Vernon had sacrificed or caused to die from his other illegal activities. Some had, no doubt, abandoned revenge and gone on to their final rest. Others likely faded into a faint shadow of self, unable to take action.

That still left an angry host that descended on Vernon before the witch even had a chance to fire a salvo in self-defense. The furious hiss of hundreds of voices echoed in the old factory that had been a killing ground for so long.

Then Vernon began to scream.

Seth barely registered the sounds, still caught in the magic's trance, feeling its power and the taint of its dark origin. He heard the babble of distant voices as the ghosts swept around him, and much farther away he thought he heard people shouting, but he struggled to remember why it mattered.

"We will end this," a disembodied voice said aloud.

Seth recognized the faces of two ghosts who appeared in front of him: Henry and Paul, Pax's father and grandfather. "Save Pax," Henry told him, making eye contact for a split second before his ghostly visage faded and he swept off with the rest of the undead horde.

Far away, music reached a crescendo, storm winds howled, and voices entreated Seth to abandon the spelled knife before it was too late.

Not until it's done, he promised himself.

As Seth stared into the area Vernon had prepared for the ritual, he saw the air stir. A sparkling red light appeared, changing from a pinprick to an orb and then to a disk that grew until it became the portal to a rift in time and space that allowed the witch-disciple to reach his trapped master and steal a portion of his sustaining energy.

Seth had seen the portal before, but during those attacks, the rituals were closer to completion. This time, Vernon's coven was out of the fight, and Vernon himself was struggling to stay alive.

Seth had never fought a disciple without Evan beside him, even that first time when Evan was the sacrifice. Now, Seth hoped that the support of friends and Evan's participation in the music magic would be enough.

Seth knew he couldn't last much longer using the dark magic and the spelled knife. He barely seemed tethered to his body, and all that he felt was aching, bone-deep cold, but when it came to closing the rift, timing mattered. He had to get it right.

He felt the battle between light and dark magic like fire in his blood. Rowan and Teag sent salvos against the portal, while Tristan made sure the ghosts kept up their attack, forcing Vernon to draw on all his power to keep the connection open. All that helped Seth focus on killing the witch-disciple.

Seth surged forward, burying the bespelled knife in Vernon's chest.

The portal's light flared, and its diameter fluctuated wildly.

"No!" Vernon's full-throated scream echoed in the abandoned factory. His coven was dead, his sacrifice rescued, and now, with his revenge against Evan foiled, Vernon screamed his anger and frustration.

Seth had weakened Vernon's magic and life force, and now he felt a pull from the rift and fought against it with all his strength. The portal's light engulfed Vernon, dragging him inside before it blinked and vanished.

"It is done," a spectral voice said aloud

As quickly as they came, the ghosts faded.

Seth fell to his knees and barely caught himself on his hands to keep from landing face-forward on the concrete.

He heard footsteps and voices he recognized as Teag, Rowan, and Caden, but Seth felt too spent to figure out what they were saying.

"...still alive."

"...have to save him."

"...Vernon's dead."

"...not too late..."

When Seth came back to himself, he lay on the factory floor, face up. Rowan chanted as she dripped a vile-tasting mixture into his mouth, and Teag's incantation made the cords the weaver-witch had wrapped around Seth's body glow a faint shade of violet. Tristan hunched next to him with a hand on Seth's chest, leaving the ghosts to maintain a perimeter.

"His eyes are open." Caden sounded relieved enough for Seth to guess it had been a near thing.

Seth managed to groan, although at the moment, words eluded him. He wondered if the last things he heard the ghosts say before he passed out were right.

"You did it," Teag said, guessing Seth's unspoken question. "You, Tristan, and the ghosts. Vernon vanished, I presume dead. It was a near thing pulling you back. You were too close to the edge yourself."

"Did it...break the curse?" Seth would only feel relieved to be alive if he knew Evan also survived.

"We've been a little busy bringing you back from the brink," Rowan said in a tart tone. "Tristan kept your soul in your body for a few minutes there. One resuscitation at a time."

"Oh, and a suspicious fire completely destroyed Vernon's monster meat restaurant," Caden observed in a dry tone. "Lucky timing, that."

Whatever Rowan and Teag were doing seemed to be working. Seth felt warmth return to his body, from his core to his extremities, and the pounding headache that made it hard to think gradually waned.

Caden lifted Seth's shoulders enough for Rowan to help him drink from a bottle she drew from her bag. Tristan gave an approving nod and returned to the perimeter with the ghosts.

"I brought potions, figuring we'd need them if we won," Rowan said as Seth tried not to gag on the vile-tasting mixture. "Don't ask about the ingredients. You don't want to know. Desperate measures and all that. There's a reason we call dark magic 'dark,'" she went on. "The cost is always too high."

"Had to save him." Seth tried to keep the awful liquid down. "Worth any cost."

Rowan gave a harrumph that made her disagreement clear, but didn't try to argue. Caden eased Seth back to the floor, and the glow from stored magic in the knotted ropes faded as Teag ended his chant.

"You'll live," Teag said. "Although even with what we've done to patch you up, you're going to feel pretty shitty for quite a while, despite drawing from my ropes and the music magic along with Tristan's help. If you'd have tried going up against Vernon with just that spelled dagger, you might have succeeded in killing him, but you'd definitely be dead."

Teag's suitably disapproving tone let Seth know what the weaver witch thought of his crazed defense, but Seth felt certain that both Rowan and Teag would take similar chances to save the people they loved.

He heard footsteps coming closer and tried to rise. Caden gently pushed him back.

"It's just Kinsley and Nash, probably coming with an update," Caden said.

"He okay?" Kinsley asked as the steps stopped not far from where Seth lay.

"He is now. Vernon's dead, and his victims have been avenged," Caden told her. "How about out there?"

"Vernon's goons tried to chase us off," Kinsley said in a dismissive tone. "They were lousy at magic and not fully invested in fighting, especially once Tristan brought ghosts to the party. The ones who didn't run off are dead. And we'll track the runaways to make sure they don't try to bring their master back or something stupid like that. Vernon's hold on the city is over."

"The ghosts are satisfied," Nash said. "They can rest now."

"Are my guys okay?" Caden asked, and Seth recalled that their friend had brought some muscle with him.

"They had the time of their lives, kicking ass and taking names," Kinsley remarked. "At the moment, they're doing cleanup so this doesn't make the evening news. They'll gather the wounded and secure them until we can deal with them."

"Glad to hear it," Caden replied.

Seth felt certain that skirted the edge of legality, but it wasn't going to make him lose sleep at night. "Evan—" Seth started again.

"Give yourself a little more time so you don't panic him showing up like you've got one foot in the grave," Teag advised. "Rowan and I need to go help Kinsley's coven with the magical cleanup. Caden and Nash can get you back to the RV. Tristan will have the ghosts stand guard to make sure the cleanup effort isn't disturbed."

Teag hesitated for a moment. "I'm not excusing the risk...but for someone who isn't a witch, that was a hell of a good fight you put up. Just don't try it again."

"Don't worry. Once was enough," Seth said.

Although I'll still do whatever it takes to protect Evan.

6

SETH

"Evan! Tony! Are you okay?" Seth and Pax tumbled out of the truck and ran toward the RV. Seth's heart pounded in his chest. Despite the ache of his injuries from the fight, nothing mattered now except making sure that the two men were safe.

Given Pax's injuries and the toll the magical battle had taken on Seth, Caden drove them home in Seth's truck while Nash followed in another vehicle to take Caden back home.

The door to the RV flung open. Evan and Tony spilled out, running for their partners, with a single-minded focus on the need for proof of life.

Evan threw his arms around Seth and buried his face in his neck. "Are you okay? Is Pax? Is Vernon dead?"

Just a few feet away, Pax and Tony's reunion went from a desperate embrace to a passionate kiss.

Seth kissed Evan first before answering his question and held him tight. "Yes to everything, although Pax and I might be a little worse for the wear. Let's go inside, and we'll tell you all about it."

He thanked Caden and Nash and waved goodbye as they headed back to help with the cleanup.

Seth held Evan's hand tightly as they followed Pax and Tony into the RV.

"We have food," Evan told him. "There wasn't much we could do once the drone and audio feed went down, so we cooked. Except I told Tony I couldn't eat until I knew you were safe. So now I'm starving."

Seth stopped in the kitchen and took Evan by the shoulders, peering at him intently. "Are you really okay? Is Vernon's spell gone?"

Evan nodded. "Yeah. I felt it break and knew it was done. It was like feeling a curtain lift. Whatever you did, thank you."

Tony and Pax were talking in low tones as Tony checked his partner for injuries.

Seth's stomach rumbled, and he realized that after cheating death all afternoon, he was actually hungry.

"What about Tristan and Kinsley? And Teag and Rowan? Is everyone safe?" Evan asked, and Seth realized how hard it must have been for Evan to wait for a report when he was used to being in the thick of the action.

"Everyone on our side is okay except for some minor injuries," Seth reported. "Rowan and Teag checked us over before they let us come home. Nash took care of the anchor and the monster meat restaurant, and that helped to turn the fight for us. Tristan sicced the ghosts on the bad guys. Vernon and a bunch of his coven are dead. The others are being taken by the Alliance to be dealt with."

"It figures that I was knocked out for most of it, so while I'm glad I wasn't utterly terrified, I don't have a great story to tell," Pax said.

Tony slipped an arm around his shoulders. "You came back alive. That's the only story I need to hear."

"You both look pretty banged up," Evan said. "Which do you want first—food or first aid?"

"We should probably get fixed up first," Seth replied. "Although I'm suddenly starving, and Pax hasn't eaten for a while, either."

"We'll get you taken care of," Tony assured. "I took a First Aid class in school."

"I took one because it was helpful to know as a bartender." Evan reached for the RV's kit, which had been supplemented for more serious and supernatural injuries. "You're in good hands."

Evan and Tony cleaned their wounds and applied antibiotic cream and a special mixture that negated residual magic. Evan's hands shook, telling Seth just how much his partner had been worried.

"There. All better," Tony said with a strained smile as he placed a kiss on Pax's bandaged wrists. "Now let's get you both fed."

Evan and Tony laid out a spread of cookies, snacks, sandwiches, and sodas on the kitchen table, urging Pax and Seth to sit on the couch and then taking seats in the other chairs.

"Tell us everything," Evan urged.

Seth detailed how Kinsley's witches and helpers held off outside interference, along with Caden's ex-military friends. He told them as much as he knew about the role Nash and the ghosts had played in destroying the anchor, and how Tristan was essential at the turpentine plant for the fight with Vernon. Seth downplayed the narrow escapes he had inside the plant. Evan gave him a look that suggested he suspected as much. Instead, he focused on Teag and Rowan's help and gave an abbreviated and somewhat tamer version of the battle.

It's over and we're safe. What might have happened doesn't matter.

"Vernon's really dead?" Pax asked as if he doubted the witch-disciple could die.

"Very, very dead," Seth confirmed. "Got pulled through a rift. Rowan, Teag, and Kinsley said they would see to magically decontaminating the area. Teag had connections to a cleanup team who could get rid of the evidence and deal with Vernon's helpers who survived. Kinsley is also making sure the wounded get treated.

"Caden's buddies have plausible deniability since they didn't see any of the coven members get killed," Seth continued, "but they have a story explaining why they showed up at the old plant and disrupted a drug deal gone wrong. Caden used a 'disposable' gun and was going to make sure none of the spent shells were left."

"It's over?" Pax sounded hesitant and hopeful. Tony squeezed his hand.

"For Savannah. There are still four more of Gremory's original witch-disciples in various cities, but that's a fight for another day," Seth replied.

He didn't mention the question he and Evan debated about

whether Gremory could siphon power from the disciples he pulled through the rift, and if that might pose a problem in the future. Seth decided he could only handle one potentially world-ending crisis at a time.

Now that the adrenaline had faded, Seth felt every bruise and pulled muscle from the fight, as well as the aftermath of working the spell and channeling that power. Food and coffee helped, but he knew that he would need to crash before too long.

"Thank you," Pax said again, and Tony echoed his words. "I'd have been a goner without you and everyone you brought to the party. I can't believe that you two go looking for those disciples. Once in a life-time is more than enough for me."

Evan snuggled closer to Seth, and Seth felt a pang of familiar pain. "I promised my little brother," Seth said. "And I mean to make good on that promise."

When everyone had eaten their fill, Seth offered to take Pax and Tony back to their house. "You're safe now. Go pick up where you left off, without looking over your shoulder."

Evan insisted on splitting up the leftovers and packed up their share as Tony gathered his things. They all got in the truck, with Evan by Seth in the front while Pax and Tony snuggled in the back seat.

When they reached the house, Tony spoke up. "Once you take a bit to recover, call us. You haven't had a chance to see the good side of Savannah, and if you can spare a few days before your next adventure, we can play tour guide or at least give you a list of the places not to miss."

Evan promised they would and waved goodbye, waiting to make sure they got inside safely. "Whew," Evan said, "I'm glad that's over. I'm all for taking a break before the next death-defying rescue operation."

Seth chuckled tiredly. "That sounds like a great idea. I wonder how long it will take the remaining disciples to find out what happened and if it will make any difference."

Evan sighed. "Vernon had the cursed carving ready, so he expected us. That's new. Although they all seem to think they're immune. And while I'd love it if they just gave up and went away, stopping the ritual means their immortality expires. They're not likely to have a change of heart."

"Let's leave that for another day. One catastrophe at a time, please," Seth replied.

Much as Seth wanted to rest, he knew there were loose ends to tie up. He called Teag, who also put Rowan on speakerphone. "Did the cleanup and handoff go okay?" Seth asked.

"Kinsley's people swept Vernon's main restaurant and house for magical items. They gave them to me, and I'll take them to Sorren's people back in Charleston, along with the wooden carving that whammied you," Teag said. The Alliance and the Briggs Society take care of dangerous magical items that can't be destroyed. Teag and Cassidy had worked with them many times over the years.

"Caden and his people made sure they didn't leave anything behind," Teag continued. "Nash's ghosts kept watch."

"We de-magicked the factory, so it's just a rusting old plant tainted with toxic waste now," Rowan added with a note of distaste.

"Caden says that the police are taking a closer look at Vernon's shipping business. He suspects there will be plenty of illegal stuff to shut it down under normal standards, but he knows how to contact the Alliance folks if magical items show up," Teag said.

"How are they going to explain monster meat to civvies?" Evan asked.

"Protected species," Rowan replied with a hint of humor. "Poaching. Illegal harvesting and transport. Unlicensed hunting. There are a slew of normal laws that apply whether it's yak meat or werewolf. All that matters is that the shipments stop and the equipment is impounded so no one else can pick up where Vernon left off."

"Will you head back to Charleston tomorrow?" Evan asked, sorry to see their friends leave.

"Might take a day to catch our breath," Teag said. "Nash invited everyone to a celebration at Mystic tomorrow night, just for our gang. Saving people doesn't usually come with a party, so we're planning to go."

"Count us in," Seth said after Evan gave the nod. "I should be awake again by then."

"Don't cut corners on replenishing," Rowan warned. "Especially since you worked some spells that were a stretch."

Seth winced at being called on using the gray magic, and Evan's eyes narrowed. "Trust me, I'll make it a priority," Seth promised. "I feel like I did a triathlon."

Rowan chuckled. "They always make magic look so easy in the movies and on TV. Even experienced practitioners get reaction headaches and fatigue. If you need anything, just let me know. I can't zap you all better, but I've got some alternate remedies if the usual fixes don't work."

Seth thanked her and promised them that he and Evan would see them at Nash's party.

When the call ended, Evan gently took his phone and set it on the table. "You took a big risk with magic from that grimoire." Evan didn't make it a question.

Seth knew he'd been caught out, and he could only offer the truth to temper Evan's justified anger. "I couldn't lose you," Seth replied. "Defeating the witch-disciple wouldn't matter if it cost your life. I'd walk away from all of them to keep you safe."

"Gray magic has a cost," Evan reminded him. "Every time you use it, it gets easier to rely on. I don't want to survive a fight and lose you to dark power."

"I'm sorry," Seth replied.

"But you'd do it again?" Evan challenged.

Seth didn't see the point in lying. "Yes. If that's what it took to keep you safe."

Evan looked like he weighed continuing the argument, and finally relented. "Let's get you showered and changed into clean clothes, and then it's time for some of that rest you promised you'd do," Evan said.

Seth wasn't foolish enough to think that the conversation was actually over. Evan was good at biding his time. Still, they had both just cheated death, and that deserved a celebration.

Seth leaned forward for a kiss. "I can think of alternate recuperation strategies," he teased, but he knew that right now he was too exhausted to make good on the proposition.

Evan gave him a look. "We've done this more than a few times.

Neither of us is up to wild sex right now, but some major cuddling and groping before sleep will set us up for a very happy morning."

Evan led Seth into the bathroom and wordlessly showed his love and concern undressing him. Seth appreciated the attention Evan lavished on him as he removed each piece of clothing, making him feel loved even if it wasn't a build-up for sex. Seth knew Evan was checking for any undisclosed injuries, but his gentle touches and soft kisses across Seth's chest and back definitely did not feel clinical.

"You're wearing too many clothes," Seth said as Evan started to heat the water.

"That's easy to fix." Evan pulled his shirt over his head and revealed that he was commando when he pushed down his sweatpants.

Evan stepped into the bathroom and drew Seth with him.

"You know we can't both fit in the shower," Seth joked.

"I know."

Evan turned Seth so his back was to Evan. Seth braced himself with his hands against the shower wall and stood with his legs apart to give Evan access.

Evan soaked a washcloth in the sink, got it soapy, and wrung it out. He began to work from Seth's shoulders down his arms, to his firm buttocks, and then each leg, soaping and then rinsing with the warm cloth. Evan took his time with the spicy-scented soap, sluicing away sweat.

Despite how tired he was, Seth felt his cock stir as Evan washed between his buttocks and slid his hand between his legs to his taint.

"Just relax," Evan murmured. It felt so good to feel Evan's body plastered against his back, warm and wet and half-hard despite the circumstances. "Enjoy."

"Feels good," Seth murmured. He shouldn't have been surprised at the intensity of the post-battle fatigue, but it always did him in when the adrenaline crashed.

"It's supposed to." Evan planted a kiss between Seth's shoulders. "Otherwise, I'm doing it wrong."

Seth knew that Evan had dealt with his own fear and worry despite not being present for the fight, but if he could joke, he was probably going to bounce back okay.

Evan turned Seth around, carefully wiping his face before moving to his neck and shoulders, then his chest and legs before returning to his groin.

"What do you want?" Evan asked as he slipped his hand over Seth's cock and balls. "It's okay if you just want to go to sleep. We don't have to do anything tonight. I'm just glad to have you home, safe."

Evan leaned forward and kissed Seth. Post-battle "thank God we're still alive" sex was primally satisfying, even if it wasn't the longest lasting or most seductive.

"I don't know if I've got it in me, but you're very welcome to give it a try," Seth replied.

Evan wrapped one hand around Seth's half-hard cock and the other hand around his own firmer prick. He stroked them both, setting a slow rhythm. With Evan's body pressed against his and the friction of his hand, Seth's cock responded, despite everything that had taken place that night.

Seth came a moment after Evan's orgasm spattered his belly with hot come, fountaining over Evan's hand. The intensity of his release surprised him since he thought he was already spent from the day's action.

"Thank you for coming back safely to me." Evan gave Seth another kiss before he let go and used the cloth to clean up.

"I will always come back to you," Seth promised, willing that to be true with all his heart.

Evan gave Seth a gentle nudge and handed him the detachable shower head. "Go ahead and wash your hair, rinse off. You'll feel better."

When Seth finished, Evan used one of their fluffiest towels to dry them off and sop up the water that had gotten on the floor. Exhausted, they fell into bed naked, too tired to even bother with pajamas.

Seth lay on his side with Evan's back against his chest and wrapped an arm over his lover.

"I knew you would save me from Vernon's curse," Evan said

quietly. "I was scared because I didn't know what you'd do, but I didn't doubt that you'd figure something out."

"Damn right." Seth didn't plan to fully explain the lengths and risks he had taken to protect Evan from Vernon's dark magic. "I worried that it wouldn't work, breaking the curse aside from outright killing Vernon. I couldn't tell. And no matter how the fight ended, I wasn't about to accept anything short of you, safe."

Evan laced their fingers together over his belly. "I know you drew on some pretty dark resources for that spell. Please tell me that saving me didn't create new dangers. I never doubted that you would beat Vernon, even if I couldn't be there to help this time."

Seth didn't want to burden Evan with more worry, but he also refused to lie. "I don't know for sure," Seth confessed. "Teag and Rowan and Kinsley disapproved for all those reasons, but they didn't think there was permanent damage."

All three witches had made their opinions clear, warning Seth not to make a habit of questionable magic and promising their help if the aftermath proved worse than expected.

"Thank you." Evan lifted their joined hands to his lips for a kiss. "But I never want to bring harm to you. Please don't take that kind of risk again."

Seth wasn't surprised at Evan's response, although it didn't make him regret his choice or convince him to avoid a similar gambit in the future. "I don't want to live in a world without you in it," he said in a voice just above a whisper, confessing his greatest fear.

Sometimes the lengths he would go to for Evan's safety rattled Seth. He had never felt so deeply for someone aside from his brother and parents, but Evan made him believe in the idea of soulmates.

"Neither do I," Evan replied after a moment's silence. "So, we'd just better make sure we both stay safe." Something in his voice told Seth that his lover knew that if the situation repeated itself, Seth would make the same choice.

Instead of answering in words and risking making a promise he couldn't keep, Seth burrowed his nose into Evan's hair, drinking in his scent and loving the feel of being pressed together skin-to-skin. Tonight, his exhausted body couldn't muster the mojo for a second round of sex, but Seth didn't doubt that in the morning, they would both be ready for a welcome home fucking.

He fell asleep wrapped around Evan, listening to his breathing, feeling the beat of his heart, and couldn't imagine anything more worth fighting to keep at any price.

～

SETH WOKE EVAN WITH GENTLE TOUCHES THAT GRADUALLY GREW MORE urgent, rubbing his nipples, rolling his balls, and stroking him into hardness with Seth's morning wood snuggled between Evan's ass cheeks.

Evan made a happy noise and shimmied his hips, pressing Seth's cock deeper into his cleft. Seth reached for the lube and opened Evan slowly, taking his time and enjoying every moan he wrung from his equally hard partner.

"Please, Seth. Don't make me wait."

Seth pushed in, reaching around with a slick hand to give Evan's leaking cock a channel for friction. Despite trying to make it last, it didn't take long for them both to crash over the edge, bucking against each other as they came.

"Good morning," he murmured when they stilled. Evan reached for the box of tissues on the nightstand and passed him a handful to clean them up.

"Always the best way to wake up," Evan replied in a rough, sexed-out voice that always made Seth want to go again.

"Absolutely," Seth agreed, holding Evan close for a few minutes, unwilling to leave the warmth of their bed or break the moment.

"I hate to kill the mood, but I'm hungry and I need to piss." Evan wiggled loose and padded to the bathroom with a sexy swish of his naked ass for Seth's viewing pleasure.

They cleaned up and dressed quickly, but that still left time for stolen kisses and a few teasing gropes that promised passion later.

"Did you decide what you want to do today?" Evan asked as they opted for a quick breakfast of coffee and cold cereal. "We have plenty of time before the party at Nash's bar tonight."

"By the way…the turpentine factory exploded late last night. Must have been all those old containers of flammable liquid," Evan continued as if he were sharing a random headline. He rolled his eyes, clearly not convinced it was a coincidence.

Seth shrugged. "That would take care of the blood and all the ritual stuff. Fire cleanses, so it would wipe out any of Vernon's residual magic that might have hung around. Kinsley, Caden, and the others made sure to deal with the bodies and bullet casings."

He paused. "Back to what you want to do today." Seth slid his phone over to Evan, showing the list he had made. "Figured we could hit one of the historic home tours this morning, and then do the brunch riverboat cruise for lunch and the early afternoon. If there's time after that before the party, the Prohibition Museum could be fun."

Evan had done a good job narrowing the choices to ones that he knew Seth would probably like. Nearly everything in Savannah was a perfect subject for photography, and Seth was sure Evan was looking forward to taking a lot of pictures.

"Those all sound good," Evan replied. "But we don't have to do everything in one day. I figured we'd at least take two days since there's nothing pressing except whatever client work we didn't do while we were chasing down Vernon."

"We can play it by ear and see how the timing goes," Seth agreed. "I'm all for stopping for coffee and watching the boats on the river. God knows we don't need more stress."

"Just so you know, when I put my suggestions together, I left out all the *haunted* historic house tours, the creepy cemetery tours, and anything that had 'ghost' in the title," Evan said. "For one thing, those are too much like work. But I also worried since we do the real thing whether it might upset the actual ghosts, and I didn't want to cause a scene or endanger the tour."

"No idea whether that could happen, but no sense taking chances," Seth agreed. "And I'm just as glad to skip those. I've had enough ghosts for one trip. I'm sure those tours are fun for regular folks, but I don't know if I could keep a straight face if the guide embroiders the facts." He also didn't want to run the risk of picking up psychic residue from something that wasn't even on the job.

Savannah had plenty of well-preserved antebellum mansions that offered tours, so they picked a couple and scored tickets to their first choice.

"You know mansions are likely to be haunted too," Evan pointed out.

"According to some of the travel articles, everything in Savannah is haunted." While he had left picking attractions to Evan, Seth had read up on the city and its history. Given its storied past, he wasn't surprised at all that Savannah rated as one of the most haunted cities in the country.

"If we wear our deflection charms, maybe it will signal we come in peace to the ghosts," Evan suggested.

"I'm sure that plenty of people who have much stronger psychic abilities go on ghost tours—either on purpose or accidentally—and the world doesn't end," Seth replied. "Can you imagine those poor ghosts, looking for a little peace and quiet in the afterlife, constantly besieged with tours every couple of hours? I hope they have a quiet place in the attic they can hide."

That image made Evan snicker. "I never thought about it that way, but you've got a point. I wonder how many of the guides who offer the haunted tours actually have psychic abilities. I'd think it would be draining to be around the spirits every night like that."

Seth shrugged. "Maybe they have an arrangement. Certain ghosts on Mondays, Wednesdays, and Fridays, and they alternate with other spirits the rest of the week. It's not like the ghosts get a cut of the ticket money."

Evan looked thoughtful. "Not the money, but I wonder how many of the spirits that have stuck around all this time feed off the energy of the tourists. Not in a bad way necessarily, but otherwise they'd be more likely to fade away. Maybe it's a little more reciprocal than it seems."

Seth had never thought about ghosts being taken advantage of as unpaid tourist attractions, but he could understand becoming annoyed at being disturbed during their "final rest." Now, he wondered if ghosts needed a union to keep from being overworked.

"If the ghosts were dangerous, the tours wouldn't work," he mused aloud. "The ghosts can't be held here by anger or vengeance. Why hang around when they could go to their eternal reward and float on a cloud in the Great Beyond?"

"Some of them are probably repeaters," Evan suggested. Those were spirits that remained only as shadows of their former selves, gradually losing energy until they finally faded. They lacked sentience or memory of their lives, trapped in an infinite loop.

"True," Seth agreed. "They add to the ambiance, but the person isn't really hanging around."

"I can get tickets to the rest of the things we want to see," Evan said. "With two days, we have wiggle room if something isn't available today."

"I can think of lots of things to do with wiggle room." Seth dropped his voice to a sultry growl.

"We will be sure to pencil that in." Evan blew him a kiss.

"From the rest of the list for either today or tomorrow, I liked the foodie tour, the tour of filming locations and Civil War sites, and the pirate history museum," Seth added. "Tomorrow evening, we could do the Drag Bar Crawl or the comedy club. I'm fine with either, depending on what's available and which you think might be more fun."

"Works for me," Evan said, and Seth loved hearing the enthusiasm in his boyfriend's voice. Hunting down the witch-disciples was psychologically difficult as well as physically dangerous. Evan was a trouper, completely committed to the project, but Seth worried that it weighed on his partner more than himself.

Seth's time in the Army came in handy more than he ever wanted to think it would after he came stateside. That helped him compart-mentalize and draw on the psychological techniques he had learned in the military. Seth had done his best to share those strategies with Evan, but he wasn't sure his lessons worked as well for his partner.

They started with a walking tour that took them past some of the most famous historic homes in the city. While the tour didn't include going inside, the guide provided plenty of information about the people who had lived there, what their lives were like back then, and what part the homes' owners had played in the history of Savannah.

"That last one was definitely haunted," Evan said under his breath as they walked away from a stately old home.

"Pretty sure several of the ones we've seen are," Seth replied. "But haunts aside, I'm glad the old homes are being preserved. Wouldn't want to live in one, but they're certainly beautiful."

The tour site provided plenty of photos of the homes' interiors, which Seth and Evan had looked at over breakfast so they could match the inside with the outside when they saw them.

The morning flew by as they checked out the shops and stopped for coffee. Before Seth knew it, they were queuing up for lunch aboard a real riverboat.

"I've never been on a paddle wheeler," Seth said as they boarded for the lunch cruise. The stately white boat looked like something from a movie with its ornate decks and huge red wheel in the back.

"It's hard to imagine what it was like when there weren't airplanes," Evan mused. "We're thinking about how relaxing the ship is, but back in its day, this was how you got from place to place unless you took a carriage. When it was all that was available, people didn't think it was slow."

Seth shrugged. "Ships like this were probably faster than anything that came before them, so maybe they seemed like a big improvement." He leaned on the railing and watched the shoreline pass. "I love the view of the city from the river."

The big buffet lunch lived up to the praise in the reviews. Afterward, stuffed and sleepy, Seth and Evan found deck chairs in the shade where they could relax and digest as the river carried them back to the city.

When the ship docked, Seth and Evan headed for the Prohibition Museum. "I've got to admit, I'm really intrigued," Seth said as they paid for their tickets. "I guess I've seen too many Roaring Twenties movies and shows about mobsters and government agents."

"Well, we've come to the right place," Evan replied as they walked inside. They could wander at their own pace on the self-guided tour, surrounded by memorabilia from the era, including classic cars and costumed mannequins.

"Those look a little too lifelike for me," Evan confided, giving a figure wearing a fedora a wide berth. "I keep watching for them to breathe."

Framed posters from the era told the story of Prohibition and its repeal, and photographs showed revenuers dumping out barrels of illegal alcohol from hidden stills.

They took their time, commenting on the items that had been preserved, including a whole bootlegging setup to distill alcohol. Despite the era's crackdown on alcohol, the path through the museum ended in a recreated speakeasy that served all sorts of cocktails that were popular at the time of Al Capone and Eliot Ness.

"That was fun," Evan said when they finished their drinks and headed back outside.

"We've got an hour until the party," Seth commented, checking his phone. "I'm sure there will be snacks, but maybe we should catch something for dinner before we go."

"Works for me. Do you want to do a sit-down meal or something lighter?" Evan asked as they strolled down the sidewalk enjoying the nice weather.

"Lunch was pretty big," Seth reminded him. "I'm fine with grabbing something to-go and eating in the park."

They found a place that offered takeout sandwiches and settled onto a bench under a tree to eat and people-watch.

"Savannah loves its restaurants," Evan said with a mouthful of barbecue. "I'd gain so much weight if I lived here. Everything's delicious!"

"I was thinking that all the people we've passed walking are tourists, but maybe they're just working off their last meal." Seth wiped sauce from his cheek after a particularly messy bite of his sandwich.

The casual pace was a strange transition from the danger of the past few days. Seth reminded himself that they could go slow, since for once no one was chasing them and nobody's life hung in the balance.

"I've already got the tickets for tomorrow, so we don't have to worry about getting anywhere too early," Evan told him as they finished their meals and chucked the plates into a nearby trashcan. "I'm trying to make this as chill as possible."

"Thank you. I think we both need that." There might have been a time when Seth resisted admitting he needed a break, but Evan had gotten him past that.

They headed for Mystic as the sun set.

"Caden and the others are in the back room," Nash greeted them from behind the bar. "Go join them. I'll be with you as soon as I wrap up a couple of things."

Seth and Evan ordered drinks and then wandered toward the private room. Caden, Teag, Tristan, and Rowan greeted them when they entered.

"Glad you made it," Caden said. "I'm the unofficial host while Nash does his bar stuff, so come on in, fix yourselves a plate, and say hi to everyone."

The snack buffet in the center of the room held serving trays of charcuterie, nachos, stuffed jalapeños, avocado fries, and more. Pitchers of orange punch sat at the end of the table with glasses.

"That's a Savannah concoction, Chatham Artillery Punch," Caden told them. "Brandy, whiskey, rum, champagne, and lemons, plus sugar. Treat it with respect—it'll knock you flat on your ass if you're not careful!"

Seth and Evan filled plates, and Evan took a glass of the punch before heading to join Rowan, Tristan, and Teag at a nearby table. Seth stuck to soda and only had a taste of Evan's drink since he had to drive back to the RV.

"Recover from yesterday?" Teag asked as they sat.

"Mostly," Seth replied, and Evan nodded in agreement. "Took it easy this morning, slept in, then did some sightseeing. It was nice to have downtime. Doesn't happen very often."

Over in the corner, someone played guitar, working their way through a popular list of hits across the years quietly enough that conversation didn't come to a halt.

"I will fully admit to not getting up before noon." Teag bit into a stuffed jalapeño. "I've learned my lesson with reaction headaches."

Rowan nodded. She sipped her drink and nibbled a few nachos. "I took my time getting up and about. We threw a lot of energy around last night. That takes time to replenish. No sense going back to Charleston and being completely wiped out."

"The energy in the city should feel a lot lighter, even for people who aren't 'sensitive' to spirits," Tristan said. "We helped a lot of ghosts get their vengeance and pass on. That makes a difference."

"Thanks again for taking that awful carving back to Charleston," Evan said and suppressed a shiver. "I'm glad Cassidy has ways of getting rid of things like that."

"You'd be surprised how often things like that come into Trifles and Folly," Rowan replied. "Sorren and Donnelly make sure they're taken care of—permanently."

Caden joined them with a full plate of goodies. "Can I talk shop long enough to give you an update?"

"Sure," Seth said and the others nodded.

"Raids were carried out at Vernon's main restaurant on wage and hour law violations plus health code, so it's shut down permanently," Caden told them.

"Then the feds raided Vernon's cargo ships," Caden said. "Turns out his import/export company had some serious lapses in their paperwork. They found a lot of questionable items like unidentified meat, questionable ingredients for magic and gourmet consumption, as well as ritual items of dubious provenance. Looks like he transported cargo for some of the other witch-disciples, so he was involved in para-pharmaceuticals and trafficking, which should link back to the disciples you've dealt with, and might cause problems for the ones still on the list. But it's all shut down now. The police got an anonymous tip that the monster restaurant was using horse and illegal game meat," Caden continued, and the little smile on his face gave Seth a clue about who might have made the report.

"The monster restaurant had a 'suspicious' fire and burned to the ground. No one could find any payroll records. And the old turpentine plant Vernon used for his ritual blew up last night," he added.

"Just to be absolutely certain that all the supernatural energy is wrapped up, Sorren and Donnelly will drive down and make sure everything is shut down properly," Teag added. "No loose ends."

"So, it's over?" Evan sounded like he was afraid to believe the good news.

Caden and Seth nodded. "Vernon's dead, the sacrifice wasn't made, the ghosts moved on, and his coven members are dead or with the Alliance awaiting judgment," Seth said.

"I'll update Cassidy," Teag said. "She'll be glad to hear it."

"Psst," Rowan got their attention and jerked her head toward the stage. "I think something is going to happen."

Tony had replaced the previous guitar player. Pax sat at the table nearest the stage, with eyes only for his boyfriend.

Tony played a couple of upbeat tunes that got the small group of guests smiling and tapping their toes to the familiar, happy songs. Once he had their attention, Tony pivoted to a popular love song, and his gaze honed in on Pax, who seemed to be completely wrapped up in the song.

When he finished and the applause died down, Tony set the guitar down and looked to the small group of rescuers. "Thank you all for everything you risked, everything you did to save the man I love. I'm grateful beyond words.

"But I also realized that time waits for no one. There's no perfect time to ask this, but Pax, will you marry me?"

Pax gave a delighted squeal and rushed toward Tony, who caught him in his arms, kissed him, and twirled him around. Everyone in the room clapped and cheered.

"Yes, definitely yes," Pax said when they finally separated. "Forever yes."

Nash signaled a server, who brought goblets of champagne for the group. "This round is on the house," he announced as everyone took a glass.

"To Pax and Tony. May your love always shine brightly." Nash raised a toast. The others called out their congratulations as they lifted their glasses in a salute. Pax and Tony beamed, holding each other's goblets as they drank.

Seth snuck a look at Evan, who was clapping and happily caught up in the moment. *I want that for us someday. When the hunt for the witch-disciples is over. It seems like tempting fate to get married before the quest is done, though. I want a happily-ever-after with Evan, where we buy a real house, get a dog, and live out a quiet, monster-free rest of our lives.*

I've made assumptions, but we haven't really talked about it. I know Evan's in it for the long haul, for life. Does he want to get married sooner — or at all? Not everyone wants a ring, but I've always thought it would be nice. Not as much staking my claim as making a promise.

It's a talk we need to have. Just to make sure we're both on the same page. Things have been happening so fast since we got together; it seems like we're always running for our lives. Maybe this little break we're taking is the perfect opportunity.

Everyone moved to cluster around Pax and Tony, sharing hugs and well-wishes along with joking advice and good-natured teasing. The happy couple beamed.

Evan elbowed him. "You know, a week ago Pax and Tony hadn't met any of us, and now it's like we've all been lifelong friends."

"Getting rescued from the diabolical clutches of an evil witch is a real ice breaker," Seth replied, managing to keep a straight face.

Eventually, people drifted back to their tables. Pax and Tony caught Seth and Evan before they sat down again. "Thank you again," Tony said. "I'm sorry I didn't believe you right away."

"It's definitely a truth is stranger than fiction kind of story," Seth replied. "Even when people have wondered about the deaths in their families, there's a big leap from 'died under odd circumstances' to 'sacrificed by an immortal killer witch.'"

"True," Pax agreed. "But thank you for sticking around and saving my ass."

"I second that thank you," Tony replied, slipping an arm around his fiancé. "I can't believe this is what you do all the time."

Seth and Evan exchanged a look and both shrugged. "Not exactly on either of our career plans, but we have a chance to put something right and stop bad things from happening. So here we are."

"Do you know where you're heading after this?" Pax asked.

Seth shook his head. He and Evan only had a few of the witch-disciples left to tackle, but where they would go next would depend on what their research turned up. He needed to check in with Milo and see if he had anything new for them.

"It's a short list, but we haven't picked one yet," Evan said. "We'll figure it out."

"Did you see some of the sights?" Tony and Pax followed them back to the table, and a waiter took new drink orders.

Seth and Evan took turns filling them in on what sightseeing they had done earlier in the day and which historic locations they were heading to the next day.

"You've definitely hit my top picks that I'd suggest to someone coming here for the first time who didn't have a long stay," Tony replied. "Savannah really does have something for everyone."

The next few hours passed surprisingly fast, a rare opportunity for a night out with friends. Seth didn't realize how much he missed those outings, something their current life didn't frequently offer an opportunity to enjoy.

Maybe we can chase down the bad guys and manage a little more downtime between life-threatening adventures, he thought.

"Let us know if any of your other witches are in the Charleston area," Teag said to Kinsley as he and Rowan headed back to where they were staying. "We're happy to help in person if we can, and always with lore and research."

"Thank you," Seth told their friends as they shook hands. "And if you need anything we've researched, just call."

Pax and Tony slipped away next, clearly lost in each other and ready to celebrate their engagement. Before they headed out, they thanked Nash and Caden, then hugged Seth and Evan. After that, Kinsley and Tristan said farewell.

"Don't be strangers," Kinsley told Seth and Evan, and Tristan nodded his agreement. "Call us if we can help."

"Guess we've closed the party," Seth joked as he and Evan went to say goodbye to Caden and Nash. "You were both awesome wingmen. We couldn't have done it without you."

"You seem to have eliminating crazy witches down to a science," Caden said. "I'm grateful for anything that makes Savannah a safer place to live. We've got one less serial killer because of you. That makes me a very happy cop."

Seth and Evan agreed to stay in touch with Caden and Nash and then drove back to where the RV was parked. Seth couldn't help thinking about the commitment Pax and Tony made, and how much he wanted the same with Evan.

"Penny for your thoughts," Evan said as they walked into the travel trailer.

As soon as Seth locked the door behind them, he pulled Evan into his arms and kissed him deep and slow.

"Okay," Evan said, drawing the word out when they drew back. "I kinda figured that was on the menu for tonight…"

"When all this is over, do you want to get married?" Seth blurted and found himself holding his breath.

He watched a range of expressions cross Evan's face as he processed the question. "Married?"

"Not right now maybe or until we finish the job," Seth hurried to clarify. "But in the end, when we're done, we talked about settling down somewhere. Getting a real house. Not chasing monsters anymore. That's when we could, you know, make it official."

"Did you just ask me to marry you?" Evan's lips flirted with a sexy smile.

"I guess so. If you want to. Yes." Seth didn't expect his heart to beat like he was facing down a rampaging dark witch.

"Yes. Definitely yes." Evan threw his arms around Seth and kissed him breathless. "I didn't know whether you were holding back until we were done with the disciples, or just not the marrying kind," Evan said.

Seth chuckled. "And here I was, worried that you'd have all kinds of reasons to wait even just to get engaged." He sobered. "I just worked up the nerve seeing Pax and Tony tonight. I don't have rings yet. Sorry."

Evan leaned in for another kiss that went straight to Seth's cock. "We've got plenty of time for that. Why don't we go seal the deal the old-fashioned way by fucking like bunnies?"

"You romantic devil, you," Seth replied.

They shed their clothing before they got to the bedroom and fell onto the bed together, busy with lips and hands. Evan rolled them so Seth was on top, settling between his legs.

"Want to feel you as deep as you can go," Evan murmured close to Seth's ear. One hand tweaked Seth's nipple while the other primed Seth's stiff cock.

"Need to get you ready," Seth replied, but Evan gave him a knowing grin.

"I kinda figured we'd get busy when we got home, so I put a plug in," Evan told him. "I'm all ready for you."

Seth grinned. "I like how you think." He eased the plug out of Evan's pert ass, slicked his own cock with lube, and shifted into position. Sliding into Evan's hot, tight hole made Seth groan with pleasure.

"That's it. Let me feel you," Evan murmured, moving so Seth penetrated even deeper. "Make it so I feel you in the morning."

Seth leaned down to plunder Evan's mouth, kissing him deep and slow as he set up a rhythm with his hips. Evan held on tightly to Seth's shoulders, letting his head fall back and baring his throat to Seth's lips and tongue.

Every time Evan came near to climax, Seth changed the pace, drawing out their pleasure until Evan begged for release.

"Please, Seth. Please."

Hearing his lover nearly incoherent with want pushed Seth over the edge. He pounded into Evan, drawing a groan as his fiancé's whole form shook while ecstasy seized him.

They collapsed onto the mattress, sticky with sweat and come, breathing hard, and utterly spent.

"How about tomorrow, in between the other things, we look at rings?" Seth combed his fingers through Evan's hair. "Maybe we'll find the right ones and maybe not, but it could be fun to see what's out there. And I like the idea of everyone knowing that you're taken."

Evan chuckled. "Gotta say, I like it too, and for you as well. Sure. This is Savannah, we might even find a shop that adds some magic to their jewelry."

Seth wiped them off with his shirt. Despite having slept in that morning and taking the day easy, he knew the stress of the past week was still catching up with them.

"I'll ask Nash about jewelers in the morning," Seth promised and kissed him slow and gentle. "After round two."

"Uh-huh," Evan replied, sated and sleepy. "Sounds like a plan to me."

～

THEY MADE GOOD ON ANOTHER ROUND BEFORE BREAKFAST. SETH BRIEFLY fantasized about not leaving the bed at all, but he knew Evan was looking forward to the day's plans, which started with breakfast sandwiches and coffee at a place Pax had recommended. He pulled out his phone and brought up Nash's number before texting.

Seth: *Know a good jeweler in town? I just proposed to Evan.*

Nash didn't wait to text a reply, and Seth's phone rang right away. "Congratulations! Was this planned or spur-of-the-moment?"

"A little of both," Seth confessed as Evan snickered. "I'd been thinking about it for a while, but seeing Pax and Tony make the move made me realize that time goes by quickly." He left unsaid that the danger in their lives made it unwise to take anything for granted.

Nash rattled off the names of a couple of jewelers. "Those are the ones we looked at when we got our rings. They're all known for good quality and excellent service, so you won't go wrong with any of them. It's just a matter of where you find what you want."

"Thank you," Seth and Evan said almost in unison. "We'll let you know if we find what we're looking for."

"Have fun, you crazy kids," Nash joked. "Send pictures."

"What do you want to do first?" Seth asked when he ended the call.

Evan checked the time. "It's still probably a little early for shops to be open, but we've got tickets for the history and food tour at ten. That'll give us a chance to stretch our legs and wake up a little, and it should take all morning and feed us lunch too."

"You woke me up just fine." Seth dropped his voice low. "I didn't have any problem getting *up*."

"No, you definitely didn't." Evan chuckled.

They joined fifteen other visitors for the walking tour, which led them down cobblestone streets and along avenues that looked unchanged since the city's early days and heard about the historic locations they passed. Along the way, they stopped in more than half a dozen storied restaurants to sample some of their most famous small plates and appetizers.

"I'm glad we're walking because otherwise I'd be in a food coma," Evan remarked.

When the tour ended, Seth and Evan realized they were close to the shops Nash had recommended.

"Ready?" He asked Evan. Happy as Seth was to actually be taking this step with his beloved, he still felt butterflies in his stomach.

"Absolutely," Evan replied. The certainty in his voice stilled Seth's concern. "Let's do this!"

Seth had worried that he and Evan might not get a warm reception as two men looking for wedding rings for each other in a town so steeped in Southern tradition, but Nash's recommendations soothed his concern.

At the first store, a bell over the door chimed when they walked in. Two clerks were busy with customers, but one looked up with a smile to greet them. "One of us will be with you very soon," she said. "Please have a look around."

The shop wasn't a national chain, and the glass-and-wood cabinets that held the merchandise looked like they had been around for a long time. "They have nice stuff," Evan commented as they walked around the showroom. They found the wedding rings and leaned in for a closer look.

"See anything you like?" Seth asked Evan.

"I guess I never realized there were so many to pick from," Evan admitted. "My parents just had plain silver bands—I think they had the date engraved inside."

Seth nodded. "My folks had gold bands, but they weren't fancy, either. I guess I never really thought about there being any other choices."

"Hello, gentlemen. Looking for something special? I'm Edie, and I'm happy to help you find the perfect rings," the blond clerk told them as she joined them behind the counter.

"I'm Seth, and this is Evan. We just got engaged—"

"Congratulations!"

"Thank you." Seth gave Evan's hand a reassuring squeeze below the counter level. "We're just beginning to look at rings, so we don't really know what the options are, but there seem like so many."

Edie chuckled. "There are, but don't let that put you off. There are a couple of basic choices and then variations within each type. Do you have your hearts set on a particular metal like gold, silver, or platinum?"

Seth looked to Evan, who shook his head. "We're open to ideas," Evan replied. "But we both work with our hands, so the rings should be durable and not easily damaged."

Edie nodded. "Okay, that helps. Do you like a shiny finish or matte?"

"Probably matte," Seth replied and Evan nodded. Seth figured they were both thinking that if they didn't want to remove their rings before every encounter, they should avoid anything with enough gleam to give them away.

"Can we start with silver?" Seth asked, thinking about the metal's protective qualities against the supernatural.

"Sure. That's a traditional favorite," Edie said, and led them to a section of the display case filled with rings.

"See anything you like? Even with silver, you've got a range of widths, finishes, and designs," she noted. "You can get a classic band with no decoration, although it's always possible to have a short message engraved inside. Some of them have a raised rim around the edge or a texture etched into the metal. There's also matte and shiny, and ones with diamonds."

"Want to look more closely at any of them?" Seth nudged Evan to make the first move. Seth's taste and practicality leaned toward a simple design, but he wanted Evan to get something he really liked. Their consulting jobs paid well enough to cover expenses and put a buffer in their checking account more than sufficient to cover most of the rings.

"I'm leaning toward silver, no extra ornamentation, maybe engraved inside," Evan said. "I don't wear many rings, so I don't know what width would look good."

"Well, let's give you a chance to see them up close and try them on." Edie sounded excited for them, and Seth's heart did a little flip as the reality of the situation sank in.

We're really looking at wedding bands. Holy shit.

Evan tried the first ring on and held his hand out, fingers splayed, to see how it looked.

"I think it's a little too narrow," Seth ventured, and Edie nodded.

"And if that ring looks too small on him, it'll really look small on you," she pointed out, glancing at Seth's much-larger hands.

She put that ring away and brought out another, but both Seth and Evan agreed it was too wide. "Okay, let's try something in the middle." She found a ring that was wider than the first selection and thinner than the second.

"I like that," Evan said, and Seth nodded.

"Try it," Edie urged Seth. Evan removed the ring and slid it onto Seth's finger, keeping eye contact the whole time. Seth realized he wasn't breathing and felt his face flush.

"Aren't you two the cutest!" Edie exclaimed. She looked at the ring on Seth's hand, which Evan was still holding.

"That's a good size on both of you. And we can arrange for engraving the inside for a small fee. Our jeweler is very good and turns pieces around quickly," she told them.

Seth handed the ring back to her. "You're the first shop we've stopped at. Let us walk around a little today, and we might be back."

"Sure thing," Edie said with a smile, and handed Seth a business card. "I'll be working again tomorrow. We love helping happy couples make their dreams come true, so please call if you decide what you want."

They thanked her and headed back to the street. Seth felt a giddy mixture of being happy and a bit freaked out, while Evan looked a little floored.

"Talk to me," Seth said. "How did you think that went? Are you ready for rings? Did you like those?"

Evan was silent for a moment, which had Seth holding his breath, afraid that he might have pushed things too far, too fast.

As if he guessed the direction of Seth's thoughts, Evan grabbed his arm. "That was...really exciting. I thought it went well. Yes, I'm ready for rings. I've been thinking about that for a while and wondering how to bring it up or what you thought, so it's all good. And I liked *those* rings, but I think we should see what the other choices are before we decide."

Nash had texted them a short list of recommended jewelers, including one starred with an asterisk, whom he said catered to Wiccans and other customers with abilities. They had already stopped at one of the four shops on the list, so hitting the others as they walked around town added a treasure hunt vibe to the afternoon.

Their self-guided tours added spice to their walk around the city. They recognized iconic locations from *Forrest Gump* and *Midnight in the Garden of Good and Evil,* but had never seen some of the other movies referenced by the tour.

"It's a beautiful city," Seth mused. "I can see why it's popular for location shoots."

"Hey, that's one of the other jewelry stores on Nash's list. Let's see what they've got." Evan plucked at Seth's sleeve.

Like the first store, this shop also wasn't part of a national chain. Their salesperson pointed them toward the wedding rings and told them to let him know if they wanted to see something more closely, then left them on their own.

"I'm not sure whether he's giving us elbow room or just isn't into the job," Evan murmured as they bent over the cases.

"A lot of these rings have inset gems," Seth pointed out. "Do you like those? Cost aside, I think I prefer the simpler bands."

"I don't want to feel like I have to take my ring off or think about it when there's...action," Evan replied, mindful of being overheard. "Or go looking for a loose diamond after a job is finished."

That made Seth snort at the mental image of picking through blood and monster guts for a missing gem. "I totally agree."

They thanked the man but left without asking to try on any of the rings. "I just didn't get the right vibes," Evan said. "And none of the rings seemed special. Let's keep looking."

The Military Museum checked off Evan's interest in Savannah's Civil War connections beyond forts and old houses. They wandered through the displays, remarking on the events that had taken place nearby and marveling that the city had been spared from devastation like Atlanta experienced.

"It was a seaport and a supply hub," Seth noted. "Strategic value. They saw more benefit to keeping the city as a resource than burning it as a message."

A third jewelry store proved just as uninspiring as the second. Evan glanced at his watch as they left the shop.

"Let's go to the Wiccan jeweler, and if we don't see something we like, we can either go back to the first store or keep looking," he said.

Seth suspected that while those things were true, Evan would be disappointed if they didn't find rings now that they had discussed the idea. He hoped they could find what they wanted and crossed his fingers that the next shop would be the charm.

7

EVAN

"This looks like our kind of place," Evan said when they reached Stars and Moon Jewelry. The shop sat tucked between a restaurant and a clothing store on one of the Historic District's side streets. Black painted wood framed the large windows. Both the sign and door bore the Triple Moon sign that signaled "witch friendly" to those in the know.

"Can I help you?" A woman with long blond hair tied in a high ponytail greeted them when they entered. "I'm Amber."

"Nash sent us," Seth told her.

Immediately, Amber's smile broadened. "Tell him we said thank you. We love referrals. What are you looking for today?"

"Engagement wedding rings," Evan spoke up.

"Congratulations," she said. "Now I am curious. Why did Nash recommend our shop in particular?"

Evan felt certain that saying, "We kill dark witches" wouldn't go over well.

"We hunt things that go bump in the night," Seth said. "That's how we met Nash."

Amber's eyes widened, and she gave them a longer once-over. "I see. Well. If Nash vouches for you, you're okay in my book. I'll be honest, we get people in here who have seen too many movies, and they have no idea about the Craft or tradition; it's all cosplay to them. That's not the clientele we're here to serve."

Seth pulled his amulet from beneath his shirt, as did Evan. "We're the real deal," Evan said.

"So you are," Amber replied, looking a bit surprised. "All right then. What did you have in mind? I'll show you what we have."

Despite Amber's initial hesitance, Evan felt safe and protected in the store. A positive energy filled the shop; unlike the neutral feel from most of the other shops they had visited. He remembered the nice lady in the first shop and felt a little sad about not going back, but the magical vibe here made the decision easy.

"We're not looking for bling," Seth said and made sure to make eye contact with Evan to verify as he spoke. "We'd prefer silver for protective purposes. Runes that actually mean something and aren't just decorative would be nice for additional warding."

"Okay." Amber had a faraway look in her eyes suggesting she was mentally going through the shop's inventory. "I think we have a couple of things that might work for you."

They followed her to a case along the back wall. As they passed through the store, Evan looked around, trying to figure out what else the store had to offer. He saw a lot of familiar charms and amulets made from various metals, stone, and wood as well as ritual items like ornate daggers.

The shop definitely had a protective and healing vibe. Evan hoped that if they found rings here that they would carry some of that energy.

"These cases are the non-commissioned pieces," Amber said. "Some of our clients request specifically inscribed pieces," Amber said. "Those are in the safe. Any client-submitted engraving orders have to be vetted by one of our house witches to make sure that they won't pose a danger to others. Do no harm and all."

"Probably a wise idea," Seth replied.

"The inscriptions on these rings are mostly English or Latin, with some Spanish and a few other languages thrown in," Amber told them as she brought them to the case. "I can translate anything you need."

One pair of rings caught Evan's eye right away. He tried to make himself look at all the choices, but he kept coming back to the same set.

"Can we please see those?" Seth asked, and Evan's head jerked up as Seth indicated the same rings. Evan hadn't pointed or indicated which ones had gotten his attention. He smiled, taking their mutual liking as a positive omen.

"Good choice," Amber told them. She took the rings from the case and offered a magnifying glass for a closer look.

"They're solid silver, low maintenance, and the inside is blank in case you want to add an inscription of your own now or later," she added.

Evan recognized the sigils carved into the silver, ancient runes for physical safety and protection from dark energies. They intertwined among the script spelling out part of an old Wiccan blessing.

"Only love may enter here," Evan murmured as he read the words. He looked up to meet Seth's eyes, asking an unspoken question.

"You like these?" Seth asked, with a smile that suggested he had also chosen the rings.

"I think they're perfect," Evan replied. He looked to Amber. "But we're just visiting Savannah, so I'm not sure what to do if they're not the right size."

"Let's see how they fit," she suggested. "They say the rings choose the person as much as vice versa."

Seth reached for the smaller of the two rings and took Evan's hand. "This looks like the right size. We might get lucky." He eased it onto Evan's right ring finger. When they actually had the wedding cere- mony, they had agreed to switch the ring to the left hand, so he tried it there as well.

"It fits," Evan said and felt a shiver of energy. He took the larger ring and slipped it onto Seth's finger, checking on both hands.

"Feels right." Seth twisted the ring. "Not too tight or loose. Just right."

Amber checked the fit and nodded. "Maybe it's magic. Those must be meant to be yours. You can take them with you, cash and carry, since they don't need adjusting." She named a price, and Evan was relieved that it was within their budget.

"Are these the ones you want?" Seth met Evan's eyes. "We haven't looked for long."

Evan smiled. "I think they're perfect. Can't you feel it?"

Seth grinned. "Yes, but I didn't want to pressure you. I like them too." He turned to Amber. "We'll take them."

"Blessed be." She looked happy but not surprised. "Come to the register, and I'll ring you up. Do you want them boxed or do you want to wear them?"

Seth looked at Evan. "What would you prefer?"

Evan couldn't hide his happiness. "I never want to take them off."

Seth chuckled and looked at Amber. "Well, there you have it. We'll wear them."

They paid for the rings, and Amber gave them a bag with two ring boxes and a card. "These rings have been blessed by a local witch. Nothing guarantees full protection or good luck, but we believe that every bit of positive energy helps. You can always charge that up with additional blessings whenever you feel the need, or add engravings inside later. Congratulations."

They thanked her and headed back outside. Evan felt happy and at peace. A glance at Seth suggested his partner felt much the same.

"Thank you," Evan said. Since they were in public, he bumped shoulders with Seth rather than grabbing his hand, but vowed to do much more once they were alone.

"Thank you too," Seth replied. "You said yes."

Now that their quest for the perfect ring was over, the rest of the afternoon passed quickly.

"I got us dinner reservations at a place that also has a lot of real pirate history stuff," Evan told him. "If I'd have known it was going to be our engagement dinner, I could have picked somewhere fancier."

"All fancy dinners are the same," Seth replied. "How often do you get to eat with pirates?"

"Do you still want to do the drag show? We'll be back at the RV pretty early afterward, but I can cancel if you want me to," Evan asked.

"Nah, let's do the show. We both know what's on the menu when we get back, so that just builds...anticipation," Seth said with a naughty wink that went right to Evan's groin.

The Sea Witch felt more like a museum that served dinner than a restaurant with antique decor. Old drawings, maps, and ship models filled the space, managing to look historic instead of tacky. Evan shivered at the old ship's wheel over the fireplace, although he knew that Vernon's anchor had been destroyed.

"Back in the day, this was a pub and a lot of sailors came here," Evan filled him in while they waited for their menus from what he had read online. "Over time, it fell into disuse and was going to be torn down, but a local patron wanted to preserve the history and rescued it, on the condition that it be a self-sustaining museum. So... it's a pirate-themed bar and restaurant with real pirate memorabilia."

They both ordered the she-crab soup plus the crab dip for starters. Seth opted for the seafood pasta as his entree, while Evan chose the parmesan-crusted tilapia.

"Save room for dessert," their server told them. "Our kitchen makes something different every night. You don't want to miss it."

Their appetizers came out quickly. Evan hadn't realized how hungry he was until he took the first bite. He finished the soup faster than he expected, and dug into the house-made pita chips and crab dip.

"That's really good," he said, and Seth's approving murmur filled Evan with a different kind of hunger. He shifted in his chair as his cock filled.

"We might waddle out of here if dinner is just as good," Seth agreed. "Go walk around and look at the exhibits. I'll hold the table and then we can switch."

Evan loved that Seth indulged his nerdiness. Pirates were one of his favorites, fascinating him since childhood.

He had expected a kitschy, pop-culture display and instead found a truly museum-quality exhibit. Hand-drawn maps, cargo manifests, and letters brought the reality of life aboard the ships into focus as did "Wanted" posters and articles about ships sinking and pirates being sent to the gallows.

Despite Hollywood's romantic depiction, the reality of pirates' lives was bleak and short. *I guess that's why they lived it up in port when they came into any money. Most of them weren't going to survive long enough to retire.*

Even so, the displays didn't dampen Evan's mood. His historian side was fascinated by the memorabilia the restaurant had collected, and he was enough of a romantic to be able to set the facts aside and enjoy a good swashbuckling movie.

"Interesting stuff," Evan told Seth when he returned to the table. Their drinks had been refreshed, and Seth had put a dent in both appetizers.

"I'll go have a look," Seth replied. "The rest of the food is yours. It's pretty addictive."

Seth walked away to see the displays, and Evan dug in. Lunch seemed like a long time ago, and he'd had a nervous stomach over the whole idea of shopping for engagement rings and actually, finally, being *engaged.*

Evan popped a chip in his mouth and paused as the light caught his new ring. *We're really engaged.*

He had often thought about pledging their commitment to one another but hesitated because it never seemed like quite the right time, or he feared it might be used against them. Evan felt pleased that Seth had been the one to bring it up, reassuring him that he was not alone in his feelings.

He splayed the fingers on his right hand, moving his hand so that the light glinted on the metal and admired the craftsmanship of the ring.

It finally happened.

Evan hadn't doubted his feelings for Seth since the very beginning. Time and shared danger strengthened their bond, and he had lost count of the number of times they had taken crazy chances to rescue each other.

He glanced up as Seth returned and caught his partner looking at his own ring. Evan laughed. "Still a little surreal, right? You okay with it?"

Seth met his gaze with a sultry smile. "Much more than okay. Just can't quite believe it's real."

"I promise to make you very sure it's real when we get home tonight," Evan told him in his sexiest voice.

Dinner was even better than Evan expected, and he was surprised that he nearly finished his portion as did Seth.

"The food is fantastic, although I doubt they had the same options aboard pirate ships," Evan said. "Or dessert."

They ordered the cheesecake, and Seth checked his watch. "I should call Milo before it gets any later. He'll have my hide if he hears the news from someone else."

Evan waited as Seth called his mentor. "Hey, Milo. You and Toby doing okay?"

"Yeah…we're fine. How about you? Everything going okay with the job?"

"We had good backup for the job—it's handled," Seth replied, speaking in code because of the people in earshot. "But I wanted to let you know: Evan and I are engaged."

Evan heard a whoop in the background that he knew was Milo's partner, Toby.

"Well, it's about damn time," Milo said, straightforward as ever. "We wondered when the two of you would get your heads out of your asses and make it official. Got a date planned?"

Seth and Evan both laughed at Milo's response. "No date yet, but we bought rings," Seth told him. "Don't worry, when we figure everything out, you'll be the first to know."

"Damn right," Milo replied. "We'd better be. You had help with this job. Everyone okay?"

Compared to some of the battles, they were pretty unscathed this time. "Yeah, folks were drained and a little knocked around, but nothing serious. Teag and Rowan headed back to Charleston, and they'll make sure the right people give the 'leftovers' a good home with them," Seth said. "I can't say more now, but I can call later if you want details."

"You doing anything to celebrate?" Milo asked.

"Dinner and a drag show," Evan replied, leaning toward the phone. "Doing the town in style."

Milo and Toby laughed. "Wow, it's been a while since we've been to one of those," Toby said. "Enjoy yourselves and paint the town red."

"We'll call when we get on the road and fill in the details," Seth promised as the server came with their dessert. "Gotta go, they're bringing more food."

"Stop in when you get the chance, it's been a while," Toby said. "And congratulations!"

Seth ended the call and looked at the plates in front of them. "That looks delicious, and I swear it's the biggest piece of cheesecake I've ever seen."

"I guess pirates lived large since they didn't know if they'd live long," Evan replied, not mentioning that they had some similarities to their own situation. "And no one ever regretted good dessert."

The house-made cheesecake with raspberry sauce proved a perfect ending for their meal. Once they paid the bill, they drove to the club with the drag show Evan had chosen.

"I went with the reviews to pick where to go," Evan told him, showing their tickets at the door and taking Seth's hand as they moved inside. "Everyone said this one is lots of fun and there's a sing-along. Figured it would be a good one."

The Art Deco theater held a crowd but still felt intimate. Evan had been curious to see the other patrons, and felt surprised at the cross-section of people.

"They've got a good crowd," Seth observed as they got comfortable in their seats.

"I'm guessing that they have a lot of regulars," Evan replied after watching the audience for several minutes. Many of the theater-goers talked to each other like acquaintances instead of strangers, catching up on life since the last time they had seen one another. Others looked like tourists who were slightly out of their element, nervous until the show started.

Evan hoped that he and Seth fell somewhere between the two groups, if anyone was looking.

"I've never been to a drag club before," Seth said.

"I went a couple of times with friends back in college," Evan replied. "We dared each other to go, and it was way less exotic than we were expecting. But it was a lot of fun, and I've always remembered how exuberant it felt. I figured it was a good way to celebrate. Thanks for going along with the idea."

Seth shrugged. "I'm game to try something new. It's an adventure."

Inside, the large room was set up like a supper club, with a bar against one wall and a stage at the other end of the room. Round tables for groups of eight left room between for performers and servers to make the rounds.

Still full from dinner, Seth and Evan bought drinks before choosing a table in the front third of the room, a rum and cola for Evan and just soda for Seth. Their seats made for a good view, but might be far enough back, Evan hoped, to avoid getting pulled on stage to participate.

"Interesting crowd," Seth observed. They watched as the audience gradually filled the space.

Straight couples, gay couples, and groups of friends found seats, chatting excitedly as upbeat music played. The other attendees ranged in age from early twenties to retirees as well as a bachelorette party.

"Welcome, everyone," the emcee, a slender dark-haired man in a form-fitting black suit, greeted as he bounced onto the stage. "Prepare to be amazed. We have three very talented ladies tonight, along with our marvelous house band to entertain you with song and frivolity, and a dance party once the stage show concludes. Freshen your drinks, powder your noses, and get ready to be awesome!"

The audience clapped and shouted, and Evan felt himself getting caught up in the excitement. He smiled to see that Seth also seemed to be enjoying the moment and reached to take his hand, comfortable that the gesture would be accepted here.

BayBay Boom, a tall performer with bright red bouffant hair and a form-fitting scarlet sequin dress strode on stage as the band struck up a sultry classic from The Doors. She flirted with the first row, and Evan guessed from the back-and-forth that many of those people were regulars.

She strutted and vamped, belting out the song, clearly enjoying the crowd's enthusiastic response. BayBay picked up the tempo with favorites by Fleetwood Mac and Donna Summer, before taking a bow to thunderous applause.

"Don't worry, BayBay will be back for the big finale," the emcee assured the crowd as they took their seats after the standing ovation. "Next up, please welcome Katrina Dynamite!"

"How do you like it so far?" Evan asked, pleased that Seth seemed to be having a good time. Two other couples had joined them at the table, a pair of women and a man and a woman, but none of them looked askance at Seth and Evan's joined hands.

"It's fun." Seth sounded a little surprised. "I really wasn't sure what to expect. It kind of reminds me of some of the shows that used to come to the USO when I was in the Army. They weren't drag, but there were all kinds of performers—some famous, some less so—and they did a great job to entertain us."

Katrina's bleached blond hair was piled high. With the hair and heels in addition to her height, Evan guessed she stood at least six feet five. She wore a slinky sequined dress in dark blue with silver accents, and also seemed to be a crowd favorite.

"Is everyone having fun tonight?" she called out to the crowd and got a loud, enthusiastic response.

"I need to hear you," Katrina teased, and the audience roared.

"Aren't you all just delicious? All right, boys," she said to the band. "Let's give them what they paid for."

Katrina rolled into hits by Diana Ross, Madonna, and Chaka Khan. The crowd cheered wildly, and Katrina courted their energy, finishing with another standing ovation.

"They sure can sing," Seth observed. "And I'm impressed by anyone who can walk in those heels."

Chloe Cadillac was the third and final performer, and she did a series of Aretha Franklin's greatest hits, which got the audience dancing in their seats. Before the finale, she paused and looked straight at Seth and Evan.

"Now I have it on good authority from a friend of mine that congratulations are in order," Chloe said with a wink in Seth and Evan's direction. "I won't name names, but there's at least one couple here celebrating their engagement. Let's give them a big round of applause!"

Evan felt his cheeks color, sure that despite not being pointed out to the crowd, everyone could tell from his reaction. Seth looked wary, but when no threat emerged, he seemed pleased and smiled.

"Well, that's it. We're drag bar famous," Evan murmured to Seth when the applause died down.

"Want to bet Nash is the informant?" Seth replied, and Evan nodded, coming to the same conclusion. He also felt sure that Nash wouldn't have done anything to draw attention to them if he had thought the club wasn't a safe space.

BayBay, Katrina, and Chloe all came back on stage for a medley of seventies disco hits. The crowd was on their feet dancing at their seats as the singers and the band turned in a fantastic final performance. The three divas took multiple bows and threw kisses to the audience before escaping behind the curtain. The band played a final number as the emcee returned. Stage techs pushed a DJ's setup onto the stage, and the band slipped behind the curtain.

"Glad everyone enjoyed the show," he called out and got a raucous response. "Now for your dancing pleasure, give it up for DJ Spinamax!"

Some of the audience slipped out the back, but most moved down to the dance floor in front of the stage. Seth and Evan chose a spot where they had a wall behind them so they could watch for danger, although Evan felt safer than usual in public with this audience.

"I forgot how good a dancer you are," Evan said after they stepped back to catch their breath. Going out on the town was a rarity. Usually, they slow danced to a favorite song or two in the RV, but none of the bars where they stopped between jobs were likely to be chill with them dancing together.

"You're pretty good yourself." Seth wiped a hand across his forehead.

They enjoyed the music, staying for a few more dances, and left just after midnight.

Seth and Evan tumbled through the door to the RV, tired, sweaty, and exuberant. Evan kept looking down at the ring on his hand, still thinking he had imagined the whole thing.

He arched his head back as Seth nuzzled his neck. "How about we take showers to get the club smell off and then celebrate on our own?" Seth growled in a voice that sent heat straight to Evan's groin.

"Sounds good to me." The club was non-smoking, but that many people pressed into close quarters left a residue of sweat and mingled cologne that Evan eagerly wanted to wash away.

Seth and Evan barely toweled off before Seth walked Evan backward toward the bed, and they fell together on the mattress, touching and kissing.

"Mine." Seth pulled Evan close to him and kissed him on the mouth before letting his lips graze down Evan's jaw and neck.

"Yours. Always." Evan arched in Seth's arms. "And you're mine."

"Forever." Seth made sure his ring scraped gently against Evan's skin, sending a shiver.

Evan let Seth take the lead, but he responded to every touch and kiss with his own, letting Seth know with his fingers, lips, and tongue how much he loved him beyond any doubt. They had worked off the nervous energy of the day at the club, which left them with quiet passion and the need to seal the promise with their bodies that they had made with their words and the rings.

Evan felt like he was exploring Seth's body for the first time, as if their commitment had made a subtle but real shift, even in their lovemaking.

Seth maneuvered them into position for a sixty-nine, one of Evan's favorites. He loved being able to lavish attention on Seth's cock, balls, taint, and hole while simultaneously being driven wild as Seth returned the favor.

The scent and taste of his lover had Evan hard and dripping when Seth barely got started. Evan buried his face between Seth's legs, licking and sucking and drawing out the most delicious gasps. Minutes later, he had to struggle to concentrate as Seth did the same, rolling Evan's balls in his mouth and tonguing the sensitive skin before going down on him in one movement.

Evan sank his fingers into Seth's firm ass cheeks, groping him as he moved to eat out his hole. He chuckled to himself thinking how unsure Seth had been when Evan had first offered to do that, and how much Seth had come to enjoy giving and receiving.

He drew back, barely able to think straight with the way Seth gave head. Evan worked one finger into Seth's tight ass, drawing a muffled moan in response. He took Seth's cock in his mouth as he worked his finger in and out, making room for two and then three as Seth did the same for him.

They had enough experience with each other's bodies by now to know their limits, and Evan knew they were both close to coming. Seth's tongue did its magic on the head of Evan's prick, and that was it, pushing Evan over the edge. Seth's body trembled as Evan sucked hard, and then he was spilling his load down Evan's willing throat.

Evan thought he might have whited out for a second with the intensity of his climax. He came back to his senses with Seth carefully repositioning himself so he could wipe them down with a T-shirt.

"Ready for round two?" Seth teased, his voice huskier than usual after deep throating Evan.

"Give me a minute." Evan drew Seth in for a kiss. "I want to enjoy the buzz."

They lay tangled together in silence, sated and sweaty. Evan felt so boneless that he wasn't sure he could rouse for a second round, but Seth kissed and stroked him back to fully hard in a surprisingly short time.

"Top or bottom?" Seth licked Evan's ear.

"Bottom. Gonna let you do all the work," Evan joked.

Seth rolled them over and slipped an arm around Evan's waist, pulling him to be on his elbows and knees. He slicked up his cock and slipped his fingers back into Evan's already-open hole, hooking his fingers just so to stroke his prostate and sending shivers through Evan's body.

"That's my boy." Seth lined himself up and slipped inside. "Let me drive." Seth set a slow rhythm as he also partially supported Evan's weight. "Just enjoy the ride."

Evan gave himself over to sensation, loving the friction in his ass, the slap of flesh on flesh, and the scent of sex. He took longer to come this time, but Seth knew exactly how to draw an orgasm from his body. Evan knew Seth was close, and it only took a few more strokes before Seth's spend filled him.

Seth leaned forward and pressed a kiss to the back of Evan's neck. "Love you. Do you think married sex will be even hotter?"

Despite being blissed out, Seth's words sent a tingle through Evan's body. "We'll just have to find out for ourselves."

They cleaned up and wiped the wet spot before showering again and getting ready for bed. Back under the covers, Evan lay with his head on Seth's shoulder.

"Any thoughts about where we go from here?" Evan asked.

Seth turned his head to look at him. "Driving, or like in life?"

Evan chuckled and wiggled the fingers on his right hand so that his ring caught the light. "We've got a goal for the second one. I meant city-wise."

Seth nuzzled at Evan's jaw and kissed his neck, a fond gesture without heat. "Don't know. Four witch-disciples left. Probably ought to brainstorm with Milo and Toby, see if we can figure out whether there's a benefit to going after one over the others."

"Eight down, four to go," Evan replied. "And now we've got an end game when the quest is over." He reached for Seth's hand and kissed his knuckles and the ring.

"It's crazy how much I love you," Seth said, barely above a whisper. "The lengths I'll go to keep you safe. Wonderful—but crazy."

"Just remember, it's the same for me," Evan said. "Keep in mind that the end game is for both of us, *together*, the next time you get all self-sacrificial."

Seth buried his face in Evan's hair and kissed him. "I promise. There's nothing I want more. Just us, safe and together forever."

"I like the sound of that," Evan murmured, taking the warmth of Seth's words and his kiss into his dreams.

ACKNOWLEDGMENTS

Thank you so much to my editor, John G. Hartness, to my husband and writing partner, Larry N. Martin for all his behind-the-scenes hard work, to my beta readers, and to my wonderful cover artists, Lou Harper and May Dawney. Thanks also to the Shadow Alliance and the Worlds of Morgan Brice reader street teams for their support and encouragement, plus my promotional crew and the ever-growing legion of ARC readers who help spread the word!

I couldn't do it without you! And of course, thanks and love to my "convention gang" of fellow authors for making road trips and virtual cons fun.

ABOUT THE AUTHOR

Morgan Brice is the romance pen name of bestselling author Gail Z. Martin. Morgan writes urban fantasy male/male paranormal romance, with plenty of action, adventure, and supernatural thrills to go with the happily ever after.

Gail writes epic fantasy and urban fantasy, and together with co-author hubby Larry N. Martin, steampunk and comedic horror, all of which have less romance and more explosions.

On the rare occasions Morgan isn't writing, she's either reading, cooking, or spoiling two very pampered dogs.

Watch for additional new series from Morgan Brice and more books in the Witchbane, Badlands, Treasure Trail, Kings of the Mountain, Sharps & Springfield, and Fox Hollow universes coming soon!

Where to find me, and how to stay in touch

Join my Worlds of Morgan Brice Facebook Group and get in on all the behind-the-scenes fun! My free reader group is the first to see cover reveals, learn tidbits about works-in-progress, have fun with exclusive contests and giveaways, find out about in-person get-togethers, and more! It's also where I find my beta readers, ARC readers, and launch team! Come join the party! https://www.Facebook.com/groups/WorldsOfMorganBrice

Find me on the web at https://morganbrice.com. You can also find me on Pinterest (for Morgan and Gail): pinterest.com/Gzmartin, on Instagram as MorganBriceAuthor, on YouTube at https://www.youtube.com/c/GailZMartinAuthor/ on Bookbub https://www.bookbub.com/authors/morgan-brice, on TikTok @MorganBriceAuthor and now on Bluesky as @MorganBrice.

Check out the ongoing, online convention ConTinual www.facebook.com/groups/ConTinual

Support Indie Authors

When you support independent authors, you help influence what kind of books you'll see and what types of stories will be available because the authors themselves decide what to write, not a big publishing conglomerate. Independent authors are local creators supporting their families with the books they produce. Thank you for supporting independent authors and small press fiction!

ALSO BY MORGAN BRICE

Badlands Series

Badlands

Restless Nights, a Badlands Short Story

Lucky Town, a Badlands Novella

The Rising

Cover Me, a Badlands Short Story

Loose Ends

Night, a Badlands Short Story

Leap of Faith, A Badlands/Witchbane Novella

No Surrender

Warm You Up, A Badlands Short Story

Point Blank

Memory and Malice, a Badlands Novella

Shine Tonight, a Badlands Short Story

Thunder Road

Fox Hollow Zodiac Series

Huntsman

Again

Silent Partner

Fox Hollow Universe

Romp

Nutty for You

Imaginary Lover

Haven

Gruff

Trash and Treasure

A Taste of Danger: Subparheroes

Kings of the Mountain series

Kings of the Mountain

The Christmas Spirit, a Kings of the Mountain Short Story

Sins of the Fathers

Kings of the Mountain Universe

Roustabout : Carnival of Mysteries

Sharps & Springfield Series

Peacemaker

Equalizer

Treasure Trail Series

Treasure Trail

Blink

Last Resort

Treasure Trail Universe

Secrets and Ciphers, a Treasure Trail Novella

Light My Way Home, a Treasure Trail Novella

Witchbane Series

Witchbane

Burn, a Witchbane Novella

Dark Rivers

Flame and Ash

Unholy

The Devil You Know

Signs and Wonders

Cursed